The Thread

Six Steps to Restore Your Faith, Love, and Life

Leonie H. Mattison

LEONIE. H. MATTISON

The Thread

Six Steps to Restore Your Faith, Love, and Life

Copyright

The Thread. Six Steps to Restore Your Faith, Love, and Life.
First published by Leonie H Mattison 2019

Copyright © 2020 by Leonie H Mattison

Unless otherwise indicated, Scripture quotations are taken from The Holy Bible, English Standard Version. Copyright © 2000; 2001 by Crossway Bibles, a division of Good News Publishers. Used by permission. All rights reserved.
Scripture quotations marked NLT are taken from the Holy Bible, New Living Translation, copyright © 1996, 2004, 2007 by Tyndale House Foundation. Used by permission of Tyndale House Publishers, Inc., Carol Stream, Illinois 60188, USA. All rights reserved.
Scripture quotations marked NKJV are taken from the New King James Version. Copyright © 1982 by Thomas Nelson, Inc. Used by permission. All rights reserved. Scripture quotations marked NIV are taken from the Holy Bible, New International Version®, NIV® Copyright ©1973, 1978, 1984, 2011 by Biblica, Inc.® Used by permission. All rights reserved worldwide.
Scripture quotations marked AMPC is taken from the Amplified® Bible (AMPC), Copyright © 1954, 1958, 1962, 1964, 1965, 1987 by The Lockman Foundation Used by permission. www.Lockman.org.
Scripture quotations marked MSG are taken from THE MESSAGE, copyright © 1993, 1994, 1995, 1996, 2000, 2001, 2002 by Eugene H. Peterson. Used by permission of NavPress. All rights reserved. Represented by Tyndale House Publishers, Inc.
Scriptures marked KJV are taken from the KING JAMES VERSION (KJV): KING JAMES VERSION, public domain.
Scripture quotations marked TPT are from The Passion Translation®. Copyright © 2017, 2018 by Passion & Fire Ministries, Inc. Used by permission. All rights reserved. ThePassionTranslation.com.

60188. All rights reserved.
Publisher: The Thread, LLC
Library of Congress Cataloging-in-Publication Data

LEONIE H. MATTISON
The Thread. Six Steps to Restore Your Faith, Love and Life
Religious 2. Spiritual Development 3. Self-Help
Copyright Registration Number: TX8 823 – 639
November 22 2019

Printed in the United States of America
Editor: Jeanette Quinton-Zorn
Typesetting & Formatting: Jeanette Quinton-Zorn
www.indieselfpublish.co.uk

*For permission requests, contact
'Attention: Permission Coordinator' at:
Email: thethread2018@gmail.com*

First edition
ISBN: 978-1733296656

Second edition
ISBN: 978-1954347007

Dedication

I DEDICATE THIS BOOK TO ALL WOMEN WHO CONTINUE TO SURVIVE TRAUMA

Transforming the scraps and threads in our lives is all about how we handle and value what happens to us. Whatever your scraps and threads, God can use them; and you can learn from them, grow through them, and find a healthy way to design a better version of yourself from them.

"So be strong and courageous! Do not be afraid and do not panic before them.
For the LORD, your God will go ahead of you. He will neither fail you nor abandon you."
(Deuteronomy 31:6, New Living Translation)

LEONIE. H. MATTISON

Acknowledgment

Thank you to my three daughters and my puppy, whose love and support encouraged me to finish this book. Thank you to my bishop, Dr. Philip Bonaparte, the New Hope Church of God prayer group, and my immediate church family, who diligently prayed for me. Thank you to my family, coworkers, friends, mentors, coaches, counselors, writing and design team, mentees, and supporters, without whom I could not have fulfilled this assignment.

"I know what it means to lack, and I know what it means to experience overwhelming abundance. For I'm trained in the secret of overcoming all things, whether in fullness or in hunger. And I find that the strength of Christ's explosive power infuses me to conquer every difficulty."

(Philippians 4:12–13, The Passion Translation).

LEONIE. H. MATTISON

Preface

Trauma has a way of following us and squeezing joy from every aspect of our lives. The pain seems to bring about more pain, knocking us to the ground time after time. Again and again, we struggle to rise, only to fall to a new low. But how do we end this cycle and free ourselves of the shackles of our trauma? Is it possible to become the women we are worthy of being and mend the tatters, shreds, and scraps of trauma and shame once and for all? Well, the answer is 'YES,' and I honor your courage, spirit, and your curiosity, and I pledge to respect and have full regard for you as an individual.

You can mend your life, and you can heal your heart. You can stitch the scraps others have torn from your spirit back together to create a beautiful quilt of comfort, hope, and peace. When I was a child, my grandmother taught me how to quilt. She began with a pile of mismatched scraps, threads, and an image in her mind of the beauty it could be. Her vision to rework what others regarded as no longer useful proved a lesson for life. As she stitched the scraps together, I questioned both her skill and her judgment. She had nothing more than a pile of messy cloth, but when she finished and flipped the quilt over, it amazed me. My grandmother had taken the scraps of discarded material and used her threads to make them into something whole and created something beautiful.

My upbringing was tough, with an absent father and a mother unable to support my siblings and me. As many families do, they tried their best, but, as harsh as it sounds, they neglected us. Passed around caregivers, I became a wounded little girl molested, raped, and abused. That wounded girl grew to a desperate teen, a scared single mom, who became an injured, suicidal woman. Looking in the mirror, I saw an unloved, empty, and lonely girl with a sick soul, a noisy mind, a broken heart, an imperfect body, and a life shattered beyond repair. I felt unworthy, valueless, and helpless, and trusted no one. My life amounted to so many leftover bits that others had thrown away and discarded without a thought. Small pieces and fragments I no longer attended to because of the hurt.

My grandmother taught me the wonder of turning to God for help, and I awakened memories of my Creator. Out of nowhere, I remembered my grandmother's quilt, and I realized what He could do with the scraps of my spirit and the threads of my experiences if only I'd let Him thread the needle. And that is exactly what I did. I gave over my life to Him to rework. And since then:

My life has become a beautiful patchwork of pain and healing, despair and hope, and fear and peace. God made me whole, and now I am sharing the warmth of God's love to empower you to lead a life with passion and purpose.

No matter how painful your traumatic experiences, they do not have to ruin your life or define your future. You are not a lost cause, far from it. Your experiences give you the wisdom to bring good to the world in a unique and unequaled way.

With guidance, you can transform your imperfect steps into an ordained purpose. Because right now, you may be:

Going through a crisis or trauma and you aspire to heal your heart and reclaim your life.

Struggle with unresolved pain from the past and need help to support you on your healing journey.

Anticipate a future crisis or trauma and wish to ensure you rise from it.

But this does not have to be the case. By the end of this book, you can break free from some of these painful patterns and know **how to use the power of intentionality to help you choose the outcome you want to achieve in situations that damage your soul.** You will explore how to trust again and know how to surround yourself with dependable allies. Your bright and happy future will begin. You will realize it is possible to be whole once more.

Through my experiences of trauma, recovery, and God's guidance, I have developed the Thread Self-Help Toolkit to aid your spiritual healing journey. It contains this book with the six-step T.H.R.E.A.D. System, the Workbook, Devotional Journal, Intentional Affirmation Cards, Intentional Conversation Questions, the Adult Coloring Book, and the T.H.R.E.A.D Audio Recording.

Table of Contents

Table of Contents

LEONIE. H. MATTISON

Foreword

My first virtual introduction to Leonie occurred in 2017 when she decided it was time to break through the barriers that have historically impeded her personal and professional development and gain skills to stand out as a leader in her field. To crack out of her protective shell and do something that would help her to move forward, beyond her past, and to forge her new life, she chose me as her Executive Coach. But, as I already knew, Leonie was in for much more than she ever expected. When I work with women in leadership to develop the skills required to contribute meaningfully and achieve their loftiest goals, I don't just focus on the professional woman; instead, I coach the whole woman. I see it as a true partnership to transform the entire woman, not only a part of her.

So, we embarked on a fantastic journey together! Working with Leonie was a mixture of helping her to discover and own her values, learning how to apply them in her daily work, as well as breaking down barriers that interfered with her self-worth and confidence. Working with the concepts from the Energy Leadership Index ™ to build her Emotional Intelligence, Leonie learned how to recognize her emotions and reactions to these emotions that were not serving her at work and home. As she learned how to develop her Emotional Intelligence, Leonie learned that she held the keys to her personal and professional success.

Feeling empowered through the coaching process, Leonie set some aggressive goals, and in less than 18 months, she improved her performance to win the elite "40 Under 40" award. She also set a goal to lead change and grow revenue in her department by securing grant funding to build new local government programs. Her final big goal was to shift her current strategy and increase her impact on the world by publishing her first book. Completing just one of these goals would be a significant accomplishment, but that is not how Leonie rolls. She marched forward to set and achieve milestones to attain all three of these goals ultimately. Now, having worked with Leonie over these last two years, it didn't surprise me at all that she would one day write a book that would be so meaningful and transformational for so many women. Breaking out of her abusive shell, she proclaimed to me early in our coaching that she felt empowered to write a book that would allow her to continue her intentional transformation; however, she didn't want to stop there. Leonie had the vision to create an avenue for other women, defined by abuse, to join her on a journey of intentional transformation.

As you read *THE THREAD*, you will learn more about Leonie's journey, the struggles, and the triumphs as she took the determined steps to break out of her protective shell. A shell that wasn't serving her and kept her confined, curled up, and unable to spread her beautiful wings and move past the woman that trauma created to become the woman that

God designed. Her story is traumatic; however, she tells it in such a beautiful voice that, like me, you may find yourself visualizing her rise like a phoenix from the ashes, word by beautiful word. While Leonie had many audacious goals, writing this book was always at the top of the list. She didn't know two years ago if she was strong enough to break the abuse bonds that held her so tightly to be vulnerable and share her story with others. But, deep down, she always knew it was a story that needed to be told and that it would have a profoundly positive effect on other women. Women, just like her, desperately wanting to work through the past so they could live the life that God envisioned.

Leonie's light shines so bright that you will be instantly drawn to her, see yourself in her, and learn from her journey in a way that will inspire you and allow your light to shine brighter. As an emerging author, I am sure after you read *THE THREAD*, you will be eagerly awaiting future writings from Leonie.

So, wait no longer, grab a cup of tea, get comfy in your favorite chair, and start sewing The Threads of the beautiful quilt that is your life.

To learn more about Energy Leadership and Executive Leadership Coaching:

www.SuccessDimensions.com

Introduction

This book outlines the six-step **T.H.R.E.A.D. System** to help you make the most of your journey. Each step is covered as a distinct section, encouraging you to:

Think of the outcome you want to achieve

Harvest lessons learned from the past

Release fear and break painful patterns

Enlist allies to support and mentor you

Adopt new mindsets and behaviors

Dream of a new self and design a more joyful life

Each step allows you to add your own story and requires a hands-on approach as your life experiences (threads) are reworked in new ways. You learn so much and grow. You may cry, and you may want to turn away as your progress will challenge. You will question yourself, your actions, and those of others, but what begins as searching will turn into a spirit of inquiry.

Please know, Dear Brave Sister, you will heal strong as you create your blueprint for your ultimate wellness in a way that matters to you. No matter where you are on your healing journey, new possibilities, wholeness, and a firm understanding of God's unconditional love for you are within reach. His Masterpiece. Ultimately, you learn the power to weave your life's threads together to start, continue, and finish the work that God has already begun in you. When women heal, they mend their hearts, lift their spirits, restore their souls, and transform lives.

Get Ready to Thread That Needle

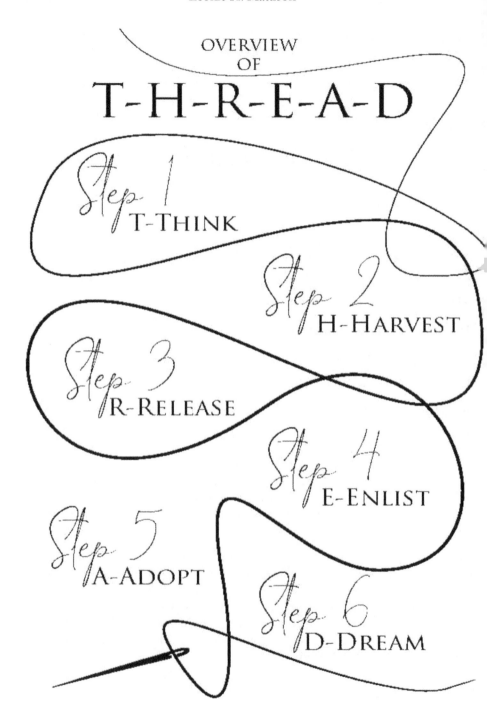

OVERVIEW
OF

T-H-R-E-A-D

Step 1
T-THINK

Step 2
H-HARVEST

Step 3
R-RELEASE

Step 4
E-ENLIST

Step 5
A-ADOPT

Step 6
D-DREAM

THE THREAD

How to Read This Book

I have divided the book into eight 'Sections' of hope, courage, and wisdom. Each section contains uplifting and inspirational stories of women from the bible, all of whom overcame tragedy, trial, or failure in remarkable ways. Their faith and courage energized each woman to use their threads (experiences) to discover, embrace, and accelerate their God-given purpose.

I share my own inspirational story that transformed a tale of heart-breaking abuse to one of positivity, and I tell of the "threads" I weaved to add depth and authenticity. God provided me with an undeniable example of His ability to shape my horrible experiences into a beautiful quilt and glorified His love, power, and personal care. I am privileged to share this with you.

As you walk through the T.H.R.E.A.D system, you are familiar with exercises to help you reflect and heal. The examples encourage you to take a step forward in your healing and your understanding of yourself. As with all advancements, it will not be easy. The 'not-so-pretty' backside of a quilt in progress is one best handled with care and by those who understand its tenderness.

Your story is a crucial element at each step of the six-step T.H.R.E.A.D System process, and you are and invited to add your story at each step in a new and challenging way. I understand how difficult this can be, but it is one of those processes where the more you put in, the more you get out. Information is not publicly shared and remains confidential to you. You can keep your work to look back on it or discard it as a symbol of letting go. Either way, you will reflect on your threads by:

Putting a spotlight on episodes that may embarrass, dishonor, or shame you. It is a false, common misconception to believe you were at fault.

Dealing with your threads once and for all, for the glory of God and the healing of yourself and others.

And, finally, letting go of those things that are not helpful, by destroying things that others forced upon you, and polishing and cherishing those things that build the new you—a Daughter of God.

Your recollections and reflections need detail and attention to arrive at the beautiful covering or finished product. You are the seamstress of your own life's quilt, and now is the time to rid yourselves of the things that keep you from achieving your potential and developing oneness with God. It may take you a month or several months to complete one step, but never mind the time. Your healing is within reach. This is when the effort at the start will determine your recovery and ultimate level of personal transformation.

Once you have collected all your lovely scraps, I will show you how to stitch them together, providing a pattern for you to quilt your bright future. Please embrace this book as your own. Bend the pages. Jot down your reflections, secret desires, thoughts, and questions on the pages. Finally, take your time to dig deep as you complete each step. I have interspersed little surprises to encourage you along the way—like a poem or prayer to inspire you on your healing journey. You will cry; you will have remorse; you will question yourself, your actions, and those of others.

My prayer is that the Bible stories, sharing my life story, and the six steps of the T.H.R.E.A.D. will bring peace, healing, and restoration to your life and profoundly greater intimacy. To get the most out of this book, be present in soul and spirit as you read.

"All praises belong to the God and Father of our Lord Jesus Christ. For he is the Father of tender mercy and the God of endless comfort. He always comes alongside us to comfort us in every suffering so that we can come alongside those who are in any painful trial. We can bring them this same comfort that God has poured out upon us. And just as we experience the abundance of Christ's own sufferings, even more of God's comfort will cascade upon us through our union with Christ."

(2 Corinthians 1:3-5, The Passion Translation).

SECTION 1

Step 1 – THINK

CHAPTER 1

Think of the Outcome You Want

"Guide me in your truth and teach me, for you are God my Savior, and my hope is in you all day long."

(Psalm 25:5, New International Version)

As humans, we have fundamental needs, and across generations and spanning back forever, these have remained the same—water, food, heat, love, comfort, safety, and security. As psychologists understand more about human behavior, needs, and desires, they know each one is as important as the next to develop holistically. But how do you adapt when your needs are not met, and instead, your caregiver or lover abuses, violate and abandons you? Is it ever possible for you to recover from another's misdeeds and evil wrongdoings? And what if this person is the one person in your life that you hold most dear? Where does trust go? And once gone, can you ever recover?

According to the World Health Organization, approximately one in three women has been the victim of severe physical violence at an intimate partner's hands. Worldwide, the figure is nearly one in three.[1] These numbers may be even higher, considering how many women fall prey to these inexcusable crimes don't report abuse. Far too many women are ultimately left in the dark, silenced by humiliation and by the overwhelming burden of blame that society often places on them as victims. The United Nations defines violence against women as *"any act of gender-based violence that results in, or is likely to result in, physical, sexual, or mental harm or suffering to women, including threats of such acts, coercion or arbitrary deprivation of liberty, whether occurring in public or private life."*[2]

Many women are subject to psychological and emotional, financial, or economic coercive control, including direct physical violence, harassment, stalking, and online and digital abuse. Family violence and abuse, including forced marriage, female genital mutilation, and honor crimes, are found throughout the world and in many cultures. One type of abuse can't happen in isolation. It is nearly impossible to see where one begins and ends as the abusive relationship will be a tangled, tortuous mess. Crucially, this abuse impacts babies, children, and young people both directly and indirectly.

In 2014, I attended the American Association for Christian Counselors conference. During this experience, I learned the outcomes of the Adverse Childhood Experiences Study (ACEs Study, a breakthrough from the Centers for Disease Control and Kaiser Permanente). The ACEs Study shows that many significant health and social issues have their roots in childhood trauma and adult health and well-being. Exposure to A.C.E's can cause damage to a child's brain, leading to major health problems such as obesity, diabetes, heart disease, lung cancer, sexually transmitted diseases (S.T.D.), depression, and even attempted suicide.[3] Reflecting every other segment of society, American Christian communities feel the impact of adverse childhood experiences as they support their communities. The testimony of survivors and ministers of various groups supports these claims.[4]

As a Christian, I've attended Protestant Christian churches all my life. I have heard sermons on every topic, from marriage to tithing, but I've never listened to a sermon or participated in a class or seminar about sexual abuse. Perhaps the Protestants' heavy focus on New Testament studies has done us a disservice? Do we lack a spiritual understanding of the truth, Christian laws, and ethics regarding these topics from the Old Testament's perspective? I stop to consider these questions throughout each Step of the T.H.R.E.A.D System.

Indeed, when it comes to the topic of sexual abuse and its impact on women in the community of faith, I'm incensed to watch our local churches treat these issues like a well-guarded family secret. Like a skeleton in the closet, it still feels that no one dares to mention the subject, making matters worse one victim at a time. However, I have witnessed many people condemned by the "Bible police" for fornication, adultery, or living with a partner without being married. We're told not to have sex outside of marriage, but what about sexual acts forced on us without our consent? Where are the teachings on this? Does any exist? I aim to discover and help you understand the Bible's position and guide you on your road to recovery.

Despite the shortage of teaching in the church regarding sexual abuse, the Bible is not silent about sexual crimes against women per se. Surrounded in the narrative of God's unconditional love—where most of us go for spiritual guidance, comfort, restoration, and soul nourishment—we find Scriptures depicting traumatic stories of sexual violence against women. But what do they tell us, and how can they help you in the twenty-first century?

The first biblical examples to study are Dinah's and Tamar's mortifying stories in the Old Testament. While these soul-crushing, unfathomable, and ancient biblical stories are overwhelming and sometimes upsetting to read, it's essential to shine a light on these stories. I hope you will feel encouraged to know that God does not cover up, overlook, or support sexual abuse against women. He is not one that ignores the 'Elephant in the Room.' God deliberately gives us the full scope of these stories in the Bible so we can:

Grasp the difference between lust and love,

Understand what an inappropriate sexual encounter looks like,

Recognize that God does not accept or condone violence against women

When committed, God does not turn a blind eye and,

Find freedom and restoration in knowing God included the stories, for;

"All Scripture is breathed out by God and profitable for teaching, for reproof, for correction, and training in righteousness" I feel blessed to be part of the body of Christ. I am grateful that I have come to the knowledge that the gospel was written for the sick, for the lost, for the lonely, for the broken, for those struggling to rise from the scars embedded by the sinful residue of trauma that's negatively impacted people like you and me. Thank God for the power of Jesus Christ not only to help us overcome the effects of trauma but also to provide the hope of healing either in this life or the next.

(2 Timothy 3:16; (Matthew 9:12-13; John 8:31-31)

CHAPTER 2

The Story of Dinah

"Christ has set us free to live a free life. So, take your stand!

Never again let anyone put a harness of slavery on you."

(Galatians 5:1, The Message).

It is hard to comprehend why good, bad, and painful experiences are knitted together in the creation of our destiny. I know I have spent many long hours musing over this one as an adult, debating with my contemporaries, and lamenting with my inner child. But I am fortunate as I have my ultimate guide, my faith, and my belief. No matter what we face, we can trust that God will ultimately work everything together for our good.

As already discussed, God does not hide from heinous acts undertaken by villainous perpetrators in the Bible. Let's examine Dinah's story in the Old Testament book of Genesis 34 in the English Standard Version of the Bible. Shechem, the son of a powerful man, raped Dinah. After the stranger violated her, he demanded she was his wife, but she hid in shame. When Dinah's brothers heard of the crime, they killed the committer and all the men in the city. The following two verses capture Dinah's rape:

"Dinah, the daughter of Jacob and Leah, went to visit some of the women who lived there. She was seen by Hamor's son Shechem, the leader of the Hivites, and he grabbed her and raped her"

(Genesis 34:1–2, Contemporary English Version).

Shechem's violation of Dinah showed a blatant disregard for her virtue, her right to consent, her body, her feelings, and the aftermath of his decision to impose himself violently upon her. Afterward, he developed sinful lust that yielded further calamity.

Shechem tried to win Dinah's affection with his tender words but unsuccessfully instructed his father, Hamor, to secure Dinah for him:

"Then he spoke to his father about it.

"Get this girl for me," he demanded.

"I want to marry her."

(Genesis 34:4, The Living Bible).

Shechem didn't love Dinah - violation and mistreatment is not loved. He treated her as an object when he demanded his father make Dinah his wife. As Shechem raped Dinah, it is highly unlikely that she would jump for joy at a marriage suggestion. In those days, arranged marriages and marriages as reparation for rape were common. Shechem manipulated both his and Dinah's fathers and the established laws to control her fate.

From my experience, not marrying a perpetrator is neither every woman's reaction nor their perspective. Some women may not have a choice. For example, even today, poverty-stricken women living in Jamaica who become pregnant through rape may be relieved to have the perpetrator be with them to help take care of the baby. Sometimes, they will marry a man who commits a crime against them. This proved true in Dinah's story.

"What's done in darkness will come to light."

(A paraphrase of Luke 8:17)

I also pray that God will expose and avenge the wrong you suffered. We don't know how Jacob discovered Shechem's wrong's, but we know he intended to inform Dinah's brothers of the happenings:

"Now Jacob heard that [Shechem] had raped his daughter Dinah. But his sons were with his livestock in the field, so Jacob held his peace until they came. And Hamor, the father of Shechem, went out to Jacob to speak with him. The sons of Jacob had come in from the field as soon as they heard of it, and the men were indignant and very angry because he had done an outrageous thing in Israel by lying with Jacob's daughter, for such a thing must not be done."

(Genesis 34:5–7).

Dinah's story shows Jewish law and God prohibited rape, to which Hamor and Shechem showed no respect or reverence. What is more, Hamor did everything within his power to ensure Shechem's humiliated Dinah further by arranging their marriage, even when she openly expressed a desire not to marry him.

Jacob was a God-fearing man, and his decision to hold his peace was intentional and not passive. Instead of retaliating in anger, he waited for his son's return. When Jacob's sons arrived, Hamor tried to calm and convince them. He promised both families could trade their daughters in marriage and share land:

11

"Make marriages with us. Give your daughters to us and take our daughters for yourselves. You shall dwell with us, and the land shall be open to you. Dwell and trade in it and get property in it."

(Genesis 34:9–10).

An accepted social pattern with women used as objects and bartering tools is seen as Shechem promises to do anything Jacob and his sons ask if only they let him marry Dinah. Deceitfully, they agree, under one condition—that all the men in their city are circumcised. The men agreed, and they were too weak and defenseless when Jacob's sons, Simeon, and Levi, attack. The sons kill all the men and return to their father with Dinah:

"Then Jacob said to Simeon and Levi, 'You have brought trouble on me by making me stink to the inhabitants of the land, the Canaanites and the Perizzites. My numbers are few, and if they gather themselves against me and attack me, I shall be destroyed, both I and my household.' But they said, 'Should he treat our sister like a prostitute?'"

(Genesis, 34:31).

When Shechem raped Dinah, there was no way he would realize that his actions would prove fatal for himself, his father, and all the men in his city. He didn't know that dozens of women and children would be left without husbands and fathers and taken as captives. Simeon and Levi were determined to ensure that this heinous crime didn't go unpunished, but their method of avenging Dinah was not pleasing to God. They should not have taken matters into their own hands, which is my message of hope and love.

If you're reading this book, you or someone you know has already come through or is coming through (and overcoming) abuse. You are one relentless, fearless, and courageous soul. Do not let anyone tell you differently. Yes, what you've been through was unfair, and like Dinah, you did nothing to deserve your mistreatment. The very step that Dinah took to speak the truth is reflected throughout society today, and please believe; you are not alone. You've endured soul-crushing experiences and had many things to cope with. It's hard to forgive and forget, and you may ask yourself, is this even possible? Yet you are here because you've survived the trauma. You're alive. I honor your tenacity. I celebrate you for the person you are. I'm holding the light of hope for you as you wait on God to act on your behalf, and it will happen. I encourage you to take heart. I encourage you to continue to trust God.

"Do not take revenge, my dear friends, but leave room for God's wrath, for it is written: 'It is mine to avenge; I will repay,' says the Lord."

(Romans, 12:19).

Keep going. Don't give up. Don't turn back. You are of tremendous value to a lost world.

CHAPTER 3

The Story of Tamar

"You are no longer slaves.

You are God's children, and you will be given what he has promised."

(Galatians, 16:13).

Tamar, King David's beautiful daughter, was an innocent virgin taken advantage of by her half-brother Amnon. Sadly, this story provides you with another example of how, every day, wonderful women are exploited for pleasure. Amnon lusted after Tamar, and his sinful longing for her tormented him so much that it made him ill. When his cousin Jonadab expressed concern, Amnon told him about this sinful lust that he erroneously called love. Jonadab encouraged Amnon's deviance, giving him step-by-step instructions on how to manipulate King David into sending Tamar to his quarters:

"Jonadab said to him, 'Lie down on your bed and pretend to be ill. And when your father comes to see you, say to him, "Let my sister Tamar come and give me bread to eat, and prepare the food in my sight, that I may see it and eat it from her hand."' So Amnon lay down and pretended to be ill. And when the king came to see him, Amnon said to the king, 'Please let my sister Tamar come and make a couple of cakes in my sight that I may eat from her hand.' Then David sent home to Tamar, saying, 'Go to your brother Amnon's house and prepare food for him'"

(2 Samuel 13:5–7).

Amnon saw Tamar as an object. Jonadab's plan provided Amnon the occasion to have his way with her, satisfying his appetite for immediate and selfish sexual desire. It is not God's will for us to lust after sex. For lust is a perversion that produces trauma and ends in tragedy. Instead, God gave us the incredible gift of love and created sex to be profitable within a consensual relationship. However, Amnon wanted to have sex with Tamar and would stop at nothing:

"But as she was feeding him, he grabbed her and demanded,

"Come to bed with me, my darling sister."

"No, my brother!" she cried. "Don't be foolish! Don't do this to me! Such wicked things aren't done in Israel. Where could I go in my shame? And you would be called one of the greatest fools in Israel. Please, just speak to the king about it, and he will let you marry me." But Amnon wouldn't listen to her, and since he was stronger than she was, he raped her."

(2 Samuel 13:11–14, New Living Translation).

Tamar's interaction with her brother was out of docile respect to her father and a genuine concern for Amnon in his feigned sickness. As soon as she realized Amnon's intentions, Tamar took four inspired actions to disrupt the silence. She:

1. **Protested:** When Amnon told her to lie with him, she pleaded with him not to violate her.

2. **Protected:** She protected herself by calling attention to the fact that rape is a severe crime in Israel.

3. **Advocated:** She advocated for righteousness by saying what consequences this would have for her and Amnon.

4. **Advised:** She advised Amnon to do the right thing and talk to King David, suggesting that their father would let Amnon marry Tamar instead of raping and dishonoring her.

Notably, Tamar did everything within her power to prevent Amnon from raping her. This included physically attempting to fight him off, but Amnon was stronger than she.

"Then Amnon hated her with very great hatred so that the hatred with which he hated her was greater than the love with which he had loved her. And Amnon said to her, 'Get up! Go!'"

(2 Samuel 13:15).

Amnon hated and rejected Tamar because she was a tangible reminder of the sin that lurked inside him, and he spitefully had Tamar put out of his room in shame. But it was Tamar who had to deal with physical, mental, and emotional pain. She was the one who mourned the loss of her virtue and wrestled with the guilt and condemnation of Amnon's sin. She was innocent, yet she was the one who paid the price.

"And Tamar put ashes on her head and tore the long robe that she wore. And she laid her hand on her head and went away, crying aloud as she went. And her brother Absalom said to her, 'Has Amnon your brother been with you? Now hold your peace, my sister. He is your brother; do not take

this to heart.' So, Tamar lived, a desolate woman, in her brother Absalom's house." (2 Samuel 13:19–20).

When Amnon raped Tamar, he knew she was a virgin and that this act would ruin her, making her unworthy of marriage, which was why she begged him not to do it. Her rape created a scar they forced her to wear. Tamar's devastation echoed throughout history, and to turn a blind eye to her pain would be to silence the stories of countless other women. Her reaction to the rape teaches us how to take action to disrupt the silence and to speak the truth. Consider the lessons of Tamar's actions:

Tamar **tore off** the shame that came from her virgin robe, a sign, and symbol of a woman who took charge of her dignity and the right to stand up for injustice.

Tamar **put** ashes on her head, an external mark that signified her deep grief for the calamity which had befallen her.

Tamar **cried** openly to manifest her disgust because Amnon did not have her consent. Tamar did not stifle the cry of a bereaved, violated woman who was in mourning for what they took.

Tamar **exposed** the truth to Absalom when he asked by acknowledging Amnon's sin instead of hiding it. Her actions define what a true self-activist is.

King David's passive response to Tamar's rape only exacerbated the situation. Despite being angry, David didn't rightfully avenge Tamar by punishing Amnon, possibly because he felt guilty for his past sins. I discuss this in the next step. Regardless, David should have protected and defended his daughter as a loving father, and he should have dealt with Amnon swiftly.

However, the crime enraged Tamar's brother, Absalom, and two years later, determined to take Amnon's vengeance, he commanded his servants to ensure that Amnon was drunk and he killed him. This tragedy proves sins left unchecked create dangerous cycles—generational curses that need destroying.

While often viewed as a tragedy, Tamar's story is one of triumph with lessons for us all to learn. Tamar refused for this one debilitating event to define her. It wasn't easy, but she overcame it through the power of her spoken word. Her grief expressed bravery because, in her vulnerability, her strength remained. She took her control back by speaking the truth despite being disgraced, distraught, exiled, and forsaken. Although her father did not offer her any comfort, and she did not have anyone to ease her shame, she was no longer Amnon's victim. She was a survivor. And stands as an example for all survivors today.

With Tamar's limited choices of either marrying her rapist or choosing to isolate herself, Tamar lived as a desolate woman in Absalom's house. Her decision is open to interpretation, but perhaps it was a radical act of self-care. Fortunately, today, a woman has more choices (although this isn't true in all countries). In many societies, she can go to counseling, take time to heal through therapy, still engage with the world, and even find love.

* * *

Both Dinah and Tamar exemplify courage because they broke the silence and spoke the truth about what happened to them in the face of potential execution. Law called for women to be put to death for sexual misconduct. According to societal norms, both women should have screamed out as the assault was happening, but they didn't. Because of this, these women would have been considered complicit in the attack against them. And this reflects the intricacies of both the law and society. Rape and sexual offenses take place in the labyrinth of social interactions and relationships.

Their failure to cry out doesn't invalidate either Dinah or Tamar's trauma and doesn't take away from the courage of speaking up about it later. These stories illustrate *"that God sees when men abuse women, and … [shows] that God's heart breaks for the abused."*[5]

Beloved, you too might not have been ready to speak up when modern society dictates that you should have. Maybe you didn't immediately file a police report, and perhaps you're still burdened with the shame. To this day, you may not speak about what happened to you. You might even have the perpetrator in your life, out of necessity or choice. None of this distracts from the courage needed to continue, to go on living and breathing, and to survive. Maybe you're barely making it, yet you persist. We are not here to judge or pass comments. Don't condemn yourself or allow anyone to make you feel guilty, worthless, or degraded. Give your- self credit for getting to where you are and allow yourself some time to get to know yourself as the new person you will become. Use the knowledge gained and the lessons learned to practice being compassionate with yourself as you take the courageous steps to move forward. Be gentle and be kind to yourself, and you will pass with ease from one Step to the next.

CHAPTER 4

My Story: Truth from My New Strength

"Hold on to loyal love, and don't let go and be faithful to all that you've been taught. Let your life be shaped by integrity, with truth written upon your heart."

(Proverbs 3:3, The Passion Translation).

I grew up on the beautiful island of Jamaica. My sweet Jamaica, the land where the Caribbean Sea's turquoise waves roll gently onto white sand beaches on the northern shores and black sand beaches on the southern shores. The palm trees sway in the breeze beneath majestic blue mountains. The temperatures hover in the seventies and eighties—the tropical island, studded with resort hotels that cater to travelers from around the world.

Despite being raised in a lush, tropical paradise, I grew up on the wrong side of the island—the harsh realities of my life overshadowed the beauty surrounding me. Mommy told me I was five years old when Daddy moved overseas to build a better life for the family. He'd gone to a foreign country to get a job, secure a home, and save money to bring over to his wife and children. I imagined that we'd live together in a new house, and although I'd never seen this country, I knew it was one where we'd be happy together as a family. Ten years in a row, I waited in anticipation to see daddy and dreamed of opening y Christmas and birthday presents Daddy promised he would send to my siblings and me. But to no avail. My dreams never came to pass, and daddy never showed up or sent me a gift. As I got older, I grew to hate my birthday and isolated during the holiday seasons.

Life was hard in Jamaica, and six days a week, Mommy walked many miles every day to find steady, well-paid work. I remember the tired look on Mommy's face as she dropped her body in the chair, shook her head, looked up to the ceiling, and then hung down her head in tears. She didn't see me peeking through the door, and in my heart, I told myself, "One day, I'm gonna make sure Mama won't cry." Some days we could hear our stomachs growl, forcing Mommy to go on long, water-only-fasting, hoping that if she prayed long enough, God would send someone to help us. A couple of times, it worked. And when it didn't, she'd beg the neighbors for food. I could see the shame on Mommy's face as she negotiated all sorts of deals to ensure that we had food to eat and a safe place to lay our heads.

When Mommy could no longer afford to take care of my siblings and me, she migrated too. She left Jamaica, as she had no choice, and my siblings and I. frequently moved, with no permanent place to call home. By now, I was gathering the 'scraps' of my life. The bits and pieces of my life that no-one else wanted. The bits that were debris, unwanted and leftover...no use to anyone. The quilt scrap I collected from the fear of homelessness was never to feel safe or comfortable and never relax. As a five-year-old, the story I told myself was that people I love always leave me, and nobody loved me because I was an unwanted little girl. In my young mind, had I wanted or been pretty and a "good girl," my parents would not have left me. This was the scrap I gathered from my father's decision to leave the family, which forced my mother to do the same. Only now that I'm older do I know this is a story told by many young girls to themselves when their father is absent.

As a helpless child, being moved from house to house and staying with strangers, I was vulnerable to physical and verbal abuse. People felt sorry enough to allow us to stay for a night or a couple of days, but this was always temporary. I lived in fear of nowhere to stay with the constant reminders that they could kick us out at a moment's notice. This creates the thread of fear that I would never be happy. What was happy? I could not be sure.

Many homes where we lived had teenage boys, and they left me unprotected from sexual abuse. In these households, they treated the men and boys as kings and could do no wrong. They treated us as young girls as slaves. We cooked, washed, and cleaned while the boys could play outside with their peers. We served the men meals in our old, tattered, secondhand clothes while they dressed nicely and reaped the benefits of our labor. Subservience was another scrap for my quilt. I came to believe that women were subservient to men

I was first molested by an older male family member when I was eight years old, and he sexually and physically abused me. My young brain could not process the trauma, and of course, these acts cannot be taken out of context and considered 'sexual abuse' or 'physical abuse.' When his sexual frustration got the better of him, he violently assaulted me, manipulated and tormented me. I saw things a child should never see, smelled things a child should never smell, and felt things a child should never feel. And these lay in the deep recess of my mind. Because of our housing instability and my existing fear of homelessness, I was afraid to tell adults of his crimes against me.

When I finally spoke up, the adults who should have protected and defended me scolded me instead of confronting him. They accused me of lying, and I forced myself to keep the assault a secret. "Shame on you." "What happened in the home stays in the home," was the threat. And now, I try to recall. 'What was said by who?' My brain is so clear with what happened, it lives it like a film, but those adults' words negated it. They punished me by not combing my hair for several hours after washing it, causing it to dry matted. They further tortured me by harshly combing the nappy hair. They deprived me of food to humble me, leaving a new quilt scrap of fear. Ultimately, I learned to tell authority figures the truth, which resulted in punishment for me.

* * *

When living with my maternal grandmother, aunt, uncle, cousins, and other tenants, I suffered from chronic bronchitis when I was again violated. My grandmother left me in the care of another male cousin, a teenager. While I was sleeping, he entered my bedroom and covered my mouth, so I could not scream, and he then raped me. My first experience with sex was assault. I tried to fight him off, but he overpowered me. This time, I didn't tell anyone. I was fearful that they wouldn't believe me and that they would punish me again. This created a quilt scrap in which I said to myself that keeping a secret was the safest thing to do. In my heart, I slowly began disconnecting my family. I blamed myself. They broke my spirit. I learned to hate my hair, body, and distrust adults, both male and female.

At school, the abuse continued. Male teachers inappropriately touched many of my friends and me. On several occasions, a male teacher touched my butt, pinched my breasts, or brushed his crotch against me in the classroom. I protested, begged him to stop, and threatened to report his behavior. But that didn't stop him. In a male-dominated society, such as the Jamaica of my youth, the girl or woman is often punished. The scraps I accumulated from molestation and sexual assault were worthlessness, self-hatred, and self-blame; I believed, as a thirteen-year-old teen, that I was worthless because no one protected me, and I could not defend myself.

My teacher, incensed that I would report him, moved beyond sexual abuse and abused me emotionally in front of the class, "You, Leonie, shame on you. You failed. Again. Come, take this test paper with this 'C' grade." He told me. "you will never amount to anything." I believed his words. I hung my head in shame as my peers giggled and repeated the words, "You failed again, Leonie." This public shaming gravely wounded my heart. I was humiliated and mortified, resulting in more negative internal dialogue. As the humiliation increased, the thread of worthlessness resulted in further self-blame and depression. My teacher's relentless and continued abuse of power caused me to hate school and fear learning. I became confused about my role in the situation. I had become used to men having power over me, shaming me, and sadly, abusing me.

Emotional, verbal, and sexual abuse during my childhood at the hands of those I thought I could trust shattered every ounce of my identity. All these soul-crushing life events left deep wounds in my heart and a hunger for kindness and love that could heal my wounds, and this impacted future relationships, which I explore in further Steps. My unresolved feelings of abandonment, the devastation of being sexually abused and assaulted, together with the scorn placed upon me for trying to report it, caused me to both fear and distrust adults for a long time. They were the source of my terrors, dysfunctions, insecurities, and feelings of rejection. Like many sexual assault victims, I was mad at myself. I feared going to school, church, and home. I hated my life.

* * *

It was not until 2013 that I finally took steps to recover and heal my trauma after I hit rock bottom- emotionally, mentally, financially, and physically. I remember standing in the mirror the first time I look myself in the eyes, and I saw anger, pain, uncertainty, and brokenness. The eyes are indeed the window to the soul because, as I look at myself, I felt like I did not know who I was. As I chopped my hair off with my kitchen scissors, I realized I had lost myself to becoming my children's mother, my ex-husband's wife, and a dependable worker bee. At that moment, I started "thinking," did I give myself away to the pain of my past? Was I to relinquish the woman I was created to be to the fear of facing my trauma? If so, how could I get Leonie back? Where and how do I begin? Because the truth as it was, there was a dissonance between the woman I was living and the woman I felt deep in my heart I was meant to be. The first step for me was to:

Think of the outcome I want to achieve.

After chopping my hair off, I started my healing journey. I want to invite you to consider taking these steps to empower you to think of the outcome you want to achieve as you embark upon or persist through your healing journey

Stand in front of your mirror and look yourself in the eyes and say, "_____, let's go on a journey together, girl."

"Think" back on past events you are most proud of.

Celebrate the things in your past you are most proud of. *For example, I would say, "Leonie, I am so proud of you for finishing that degree in 2012."*

"Think" on current events and how they make you feel today.

Say how you are feeling? *For example, I would say something to myself like, "Leonie, I feel lost today. I don't know who I am, why I am here, and how to find myself."*

Honor how you are feeling at this moment.

"Still looking in the mirror, "think" back over past events that made you feel shamed, dishonored, and the ones that created the trauma for you. *For me, it was saying something to myself, Leonie, they abused you as a child, and we need to go find that little girl and help her heal."*

20

Over the next three years, and with integrating clinical, medical, practical, and spiritual interventions, I went on a seemingly impossible spiritual healing journey to forgive everyone who had violated me. But mostly, I needed to stop hating myself and, from there, **"think of the outcome I wanted to achieve,"** so I could re-discover my self-worth. Here are some steps I took that helped me achieved that goal.

Awareness and acknowledgment of the level of my trauma and what I had been through so I could disrupt the silence and speak the truth about the trauma I suffered. For years I lived in shame and blamed myself for what happened, thinking I was at fault for the sins of my abusers. This created a false sense of value and identity that I found in relationships with certain people, things, and places. I was trapped in a closet.

Understanding the impact my culture, spirituality, and family had over my life and getting help to dismantle and uproot, let go of the toxic tie to people and things. We all have these and the impact in different ways. I knew deep down that I did not need these in my life, but I was soul tie to people with who I invested my hope and longing. But my heart was sick because of unfulfilled deferred hope. I needed God's intervention and healing from manipulation (where a narcissist pushed my sexual limits and made me feel no one could fulfill me, but he imprisoned me). This destroyed my capacity to trust and created a sense of personal insecurity and unworthiness).

Learning to manage the gift of empathy as I permit myself to let go of negative experiences, grabbing hold of the things that would help shape me into the woman God created me to be. It feels terrific being the woman who lives with intentionality while deepening my relationship with God. I realize now, more than ever, that as survivors, we are genuinely courageous women. Although others have knocked us down, we have found the vigor to rise and forge ahead. And if you are reading this book, you too are being shaped, and God can use you to help others find hope along their journey of healing.

Healing of trauma. Trauma is a demonic attack and stronghold on our self-worth. While therapy, medication, support from trusted allies, and counseling were helpful for me, it was the power of the Holy Spirit within me that destroyed everything that hindered my purpose and transformed my life. I've discovered that an individual cannot make a change without awareness of "the" or "her" problem and accept that there is always more than just one solution to the problem. [Example: Our religious faith has clearly stated how sexual abuse is "a problem" and not to be tolerated; we accept that there are many solutions to stop the abuse.] That is where we all must start.

Rising from rape, I know God loves us unconditionally, and he does not judge us by the number of scars on our bodies or in our hearts. God does not hate you. He does not blame you for the wrongs committed against you or to you, or that you have done to yourself. God loves you, and His love never requires you to walk in fear of who you are. You do not have to fear punishment for your past if you surrender all to Jesus and accept that you have a future in God going forward.

"Look with wonder at a depth of the Father's wondrous love that he has lavished on us! He has called us and made us his very own beloved children. The reason the world doesn't recognize who we are is that they didn't recognize him."

(1 John 3:1).

Like Mama taught me, our lives are just like that quilt—composed of multiple scraps held together by threads of experience. Separately these scraps appear useless, but along with the thread, they form a remarkable story. I have survived multiple sexual assaults and trauma and suffered pain. But I have since used my life's scraps and threads to design an incredible and beautiful life through Christ. Your threads may look dark at times, and they might even become tangled, broken, weak, or knotted. But keep your focus on God's design for your life and what better purpose you can achieve. With all the obstacles we as women have experienced and endured within our cultures and traditions, and how we have fought hard to not sink deeper in depression and self-hatred, I can't help but say, "Thank you, Lord." If God made way for me, then He will also make way for you. Life is a patchwork of exciting opportunities, waiting to reconnect by your threads and your understanding. Your threads of experience, both good and bad, are unique. And the God that is weaving the together knows what He is doing.

Think

Today take a
few minutes to sit
quietly
...and Think

...on what is true, honest, inspiring,
necessary and kind.

CHAPTER 5

Your Story

"We can demolish every deceptive fantasy that opposes God and breakthrough every arrogant attitude that is raised in defiance of the true knowledge of God. We capture, like prisoners of war, every thought and insist that it bow in obedience to the Anointed One."

(2 Corinthians 10:5, The Passion Translation).

I know you have a deep-seated desire to heal strong, maximize your potential, and to live your best life, and I want you to know that you can. Sometimes because of the hardship, setbacks, and constant interruptions of life, negative thoughts enter. And this is normal. Why wouldn't they? Life can challenge. But before long, these thoughts can take over the mind. God's Word encourages and helps us, as Christians, to recognize that we have the power to get rid of the thoughts that prevent us from putting on the mind of Christ.

The first step in overcoming all the things that hold us back, causing us shame and self-hatred, is seemingly modest.

Think of the outcome you want to achieve.

Let me ask you this, "who do you want to become?" This is not a simple question, and it's not as easy to answer as you might imagine. If you are like me, many of the things that led me to destructive behavior occurred early in my life, and I buried them deep, deep down in my psyche. They influenced my every thought, word, and action. But I hid them below the surface level of my conscious mind. I would often do things and not know why I behaved out of fear or acted in an oversensitive manner.

Here's the thing. What you allow into your thoughts determines your behavior, and those behaviors ultimately lead to actions, and your actions shape the life you live. The brain is like a computer. It collects, processes, and stores many events, images, experiences, and other various information daily. Many of us have lived in toxic environments that taught us how to be a woman who fulfills the fantasy of what other people imagine. However, God created you in His image. He wants you to know who you are in Him and reflect the woman He created you to be.

Like an old itchy sweater or a tight-fitting shoe, you have now outgrown the pain of your past. The emotions that once fitted your soul and mind no longer correspond. Therefore, this step may take longer than you first assume, but this is OK. Yes, your recovery will have its ups and downs, and your emotions will react on and off based on the trauma you have come through. However, I want you to know God is here for you, and He is committed to getting you safely through your healing journey. I invite you to step away from all the noise and commotion of work. Let the kids and pets visit Grandma or not. Find a quiet space where you can begin clearing out the things in your heart that have been hindering you from moving forward in boldness.

Grab your **"Thread Workbook"** or pen and paper and take the following action steps:

* * *

T: Think of the Outcome You Want to Achieve

Let's envision Jesus standing with you, holding your hand. He protects you. You are loved, and nothing can change that. Together with our Redeemer, you are going on a journey. A journey into your past from as far back as you can first remember.

Ask yourself:

- **Who do I want to become?**

➢ *Name the woman you envision yourself to be.*

➢ *Is she a successful entrepreneur?*

➢ *Is she a devoted wife and mother?*

➢ *Is she a self-assured business leader?*

What outcome do I want to achieve?

Stand in front of your mirror and look yourself in the eyes and say, _____, *let's go on a journey together, girl."*

Next, "Think" back on **past** events you are most proud of and say,
"_____, *I achieved* _____, *and I am proud of you girl."*

Then "Think" on **current** events and the things you are working on and notice how they make you feel and say, "_____, *I am achieving*
_____ *and that makes me feel* _____."

Finally, "Think" about 1-3 outcomes you want to achieve in the **future** and by what due date and say

"_____, *I will achieve* _____ *by*_____."

Write your thoughts down. Sometimes we find it hard to record our thoughts, opinions, and feelings on paper, but you will get used to it. Practice doing so. You will come to realize it is safe.

Who do I want to be?

What outcome do I want to achieve?

What does "this woman" look like? Describe her character, her lifestyle, her speech.

Write your responses.

Now think of your childhood and the first time a situation led you to feel ashamed, embarrassed, guilty, ridiculed, or neglected. What was the event? Write it. You will build a list of all the scraps and threads of your life that are secretly influencing your present. To completely release all that is holding you back, you will need to go step by step, event by event, from your earliest memory. This may take hours, days, or even months. The critical thing in Step One is not to leave anything out.

Make a complete list of what you remember. For example, after reading what I have shared thus far about my life, you will see that the first event that rocked my world occurred when I was five years old—my father's abandonment. The first few items will come quickly, but at some points, you will think you have it all and then realize there is more to go. Take your time; this is a crucial step.

Hug yourself and say the following:

What was the event?	At what age did it happen?	Who was involved?

"Those past hurts are powerless to harm me."

Love surrounds you, and the Holy Spirit is there with you and in you.

Pause, rest your heart, and let's connect to God through prayer.

A Pattern to Quilt – Truth

I invite you to step away from the pain that envelops you. Instead of fixating on the backside of the quilt, you are creating, reach forward, lovingly and slowly flip over the quilt of your life, and look at the stunning work of art God is creating. Get excited. Remember that your quilt is still incomplete, so sit with the finished product and honor your progress.

Visualize what your quilt will look like tomorrow and, once the masterpiece is complete. You deserve to live with joy. You deserve to enjoy peace of mind. You deserve to give yourself the chance to be the woman you always knew God created you to be. You can!

Beloved, Jesus awakened you to this victorious self and launched you into this brand-new day with enough of everything you need. You have power. You have a sound mind. You are loved. You've been created in love. You are a chosen woman. You are part of a royal priesthood. You are a holy nation. You are a precious daughter. You have the right to declare the praises of Him who called you out of darkness into His marvelous light (1 Peter 2:9). You are enough! You are beautiful enough; you are healing enough; you are wise enough and compassionate enough. Let your enoughness be enough!

Now, remind your heart that you have power over your mind. Be patient with and kind to yourself. Be okay with embracing and loving who you are right now. Celebrate and honor the woman you are becoming.

Look at the companion Coloring Book.

Enjoy the illustrative art and journal aimed at supporting your healing journey.

CHAPTER 6

A Prayer for Truth

Father, I am calling on the personal power, support, and resources given to me by You, my God, in the form of the Holy Spirit. I am ready to allow You in.

I thank You for opening my eyes to see that I can overcome my past and be made whole.

Please help me break free from the chains of bondage from the past traumatic experiences that hold me back from fulfilling my purpose in You.

Please also forgive me for everything I've done that was not pleasing in Your sight.

Thank You for freeing me from fear to break my silence boldly, face the truth about what has happened to me, and start anew.

Thank You for freeing me from the condemnation and shame of abuse and allowing me to walk forward in the newness of Christ.

Thank You that old things have passed away and that I am a new creature in You.

No longer will I be a victim of shame, guilt, humiliation, or fear, but I am victorious through the power of my testimony.

Thank You, Lord, for victory, freedom, and new beginnings. I declare I am a courageous woman.

In Jesus' name. Amen

A Time to Reflect on Your Truth

....
....
....
....
....
....
....
....
....
....
....
....
....
....
....
....
....
....
....
....
....

....
....
....
....
....
....
....
....
....
....
....
....
....
....
....
....
....
....
....
....
....
....
....
....
....
....
....
....
....
....

SECTION 2

Step 2 – HARVEST

CHAPTER 7

Harvest the Lessons Learned

*"Don't be afraid, because you won't be ashamed; don't fear shame, for you won't be humiliated
because you will forget the disgrace of your youth, and the reproach of your widowhood you will
remember no more."*

(Isaiah 54:4, International Standard Version).

Have you felt ruined or reduced by a painful experience? Do you believe that there is something disgraceful about yourself, yet you crave for the very thing that made you feel unworthy of love and forgiveness? Perhaps you unwittingly fall into old patterns without realizing it.? Behaviors that make you think you are not enough. Many of us do.

Most of our behaviors are not intentional, and therefore we do not consciously self-examine to uncover how our decisions create behavioral patterns that produce the experiences we have. We react without thinking. We can waste our years staying in toxic relationships, unhealthy environments, and soul wounding situations that impede us from pursuing our purpose in life. And these become habits. Trauma muddies the water further, making it impossible to know our self-worth and tainting our judgments. If left feeling purposeless and lost, how can you fulfill your God-ordained purpose in life? But do you yearn to live in joyful freedom but find yourself stuck because of the pain experienced in your past?

Overcoming experiences such as sexual abuse is an arduous process, and you know it doesn't happen overnight. No matter where you look for validation, you remain unconvinced. For your hard work to prevail and for you to set yourself free, it is not your battle alone. Understanding who to turn to at such times is a trial, which is the purpose of this book. You will have a constant companion as you travel on your journey to healing, and you will have a companion you can rely upon. However, to understand more, you need to understand the concept of spiritual abuse. This is an important concept when discovering healing within a religious context and under spiritual leadership. In his book, Healing Spiritual Abuse, Ken Blue states:

"Spiritual abuse happens when a leader with spiritual authority uses that authority to coerce, control, or exploit a follower, thus causing spiritual wounds."[1]

Whereas Juanita and Dale Ryan define spiritual abuse as:

The kind of abuse which damages the entire core of who we are. It leaves us spiritually disorganized and emotionally cut off from the healing love of God.[2]

Ultimately, spiritual abuse is like a wounding of the soul and the spirit. It involves the perpetrator recognizing a person's deep need for help and healing from God and using it to take advantage of them. An individual, vulnerable through a crime such as sexual abuse, may turn to the church, its religious people, or its communities and reach out for help. Their vulnerability may be a further target for coercion and control within this spiritual context. Churches need to be accountable and take responsibility. They must furnish leaders with proper training and the essential resources to recognize, combat, and converse about spiritual and sexual abuse. They need to understand the privileged position the abuser holds within the church, and women need equipping with tools to discern when they are being manipulated. Women's ministries are prime opportunities to address this need. Unfortunately, many do not provide the space for women to discuss their vulnerabilities and learn how not to let those in authority exploit them.

From my experiences and observations, girls and women are not fueled with the confidence, strength, and courage to stand up to sexual abuse of any kind. Let alone within a male-dominated environment such as the church. *"Instead, we are being lulled into learned powerlessness and self-doubt that leaves us unprepared to reject an abuser's words and behavior and to stand our ground before abuse gains traction."[3]*

In the words of Carolyn Custis James:

God didn't create his Daughters to cower in the face of abuse but to stand up, not only for ourselves, which is often the hard part, but also for others who will be the next victims. We are not powerless. We were born to think, to discern, to decide, and to stand against evil. God equips us to take responsibility for the situations we face and think, decide, and act, even if that takes us out of our female comfort zone.[4]

There is no doubt spiritual abuse is a life-altering circumstance. It uses spiritual language for coercion and justification of actions, creating unworthiness, shame, helplessness, and guilt. It's challenging for the abused to deal with the aftershocks of the abuse as they come to terms with "Why me?" "What did I do?" The victim must sift through the spiritual language, emotional abuse, and abusive actions to make sense of their world. However, God provides tools and resources to equip you with the necessary skills to defeat the negative thoughts that attempt to keep you tethered to the hostage of the past.

If you've experienced spiritual abuse, this faith walk will require you to learn to trust God to help you navigate through the darkness and into:

His marvelous light. There's no wound too deep for God's love to heal, and you're not broken or so impaired that you can't be restored and learn to love yourself again. All things are possible with God (Mark 10:27)

To heal, I encourage you to be kind to yourself and extend grace to your heart for not knowing what you didn't know before you learned it. Keep reminding yourself that the abuse you suffered was not your fault. I understand that it's much easier for you to numb or ignore your pain than to acknowledge and face it. But know, dear sister, you cannot heal strong from trauma or serve God wholeheartedly if you choose to hold on to hurt, shame, and guilt. If you're struggling to forgive a perpetrator, or if you have made a mistake and have fallen into sin, go to God, confess your sins, surrender your hurt, and accept His forgiveness. God will forgive and restore your faith in Him.

This section will look at the Old Testament and the stories of two women who were both coerced into having sex with a figure of authority in their lives. It didn't matter how they felt about it or what they wanted to do; others stripped their right to consent from them. They didn't have a choice in the matter. It's important to understand that women have a fundamental right to consent (or not consent) to any sexual activity. *"Consent means actively agreeing to be sexual with someone. Consent lets someone know that sex is wanted. Sexual activity without consent is rape or sexual assault."*[5]

According to Psychology Today, agreement to sex is not consent, and rape and sexual assault can occur with no force or threat.[6] This can mean being taken advantage of through sexual deceit or engaging in a sexual act out of feelings of obligation or fear of consequences.

"A spiritually abusive person exploits vulnerabilities many women are unaware they even have, often because those vulnerabilities are considered godly attributes—things like submissiveness, patience, forgiveness, and trust. So, it's easy to be blindsided by a spiritually abusive encounter from a trusted source and not know what to think, which way to turn, or how to get out."[7]

However, God includes the stories of these women to show us that:

Just because a person has the power to do something does not make their wrongdoing right or acceptable in God's eyes. **No human being's power can contend with God's supreme authority.**

No human being is a "mistake" in God's eyes. He wants every person to fulfill their purpose and destiny, **but we have to follow and obey Him.**

Sexual abuse has consequences for the abusers and potentially their descendant(s).

There is no greater love than the love that God has for His children, and **He will move heaven and earth to come to their rescue.**

Spiritual abuse is immoral, always sinful, and it's unfair. It is a deeply emotional personal assault on your self-worth, courage, and spirit. Faith leaders who inappropriately touch, willingly wounds, and are engaged in sexual sins against the body of Christ, are not saved. God sees, understands, and feels everything that concerns you, and He will avenge you. He will not allow your hurt and turmoil to go unnoticed. He doesn't turn away from you when you've been dishonored. He turns to you, so let Him comfort you like only He can.

"The Lord is close to the broken-hearted, and he saves those whose spirits have been crushed."

(Psalm 34:18, New Century Version).

CHAPTER 8

The Story of Hagar

"The Lord does what is right and fair for all who are wronged by others."

(Psalm 103:6, New Century Version).

In Genesis 12, God gave Abram (whose name God later changed to Abraham) four specific promises:

Land in a particular location

Descendants that would be righteous

Blessings

A son by Sarai, his wife (whose name was later changed to Sarah).

For ten years, the couple waited on the Lord to bring to pass what He had promised. As was customary in those days, Abram and Sarai had a female slave named Hagar, who lived in their home and served Sarai. Sarai was in her late seventies and still had no children, so instead of continuing to wait for God to fulfill His promise, she took matters into her own hands:

"And Sarai said to Abram, 'Behold now; the Lord has prevented me from bearing children. Go into my servant; it may be that I shall obtain children by her"

(Genesis, 16:2).

As Sarai had reached seventy years old, she decided the Lord had kept her from bearing children – this wasn't the case. It had just not yet happened. God had promised, and in time, it would happen. However, fulfilling God's promises were not for appointed times, and whenever we try to help God out, we only create a mess that further delay God's plan. Because of her inability to wait, Sarai selfishly made Hagar, an innocent bystander. She was to become a key player in a plan she could not consent to.

Enslaved, Hagar was already a victim. Then, as so many enslaved women have been across the centuries, she was sexually assaulted. It is useless to claim that perhaps she enjoyed it, or wanted it, or liked Abram. Firstly, the scriptures indicate no such thing, and more importantly, she did not have the freedom to say no. Consent is meaningless if a person cannot freely refuse sexual advances.[8]

Abram could easily have refused to do what Sarai asked. His role could have been to reassure and remind her to wait on the Lord. But he committed adultery because of his wife's instructions.

"And he went into Hagar, and she conceived. And when she saw that she had conceived, she looked with contempt on her mistress. And Sarai said to Abram, 'May the wrong done to me be on you! I gave my servant to your embrace, and when she saw that she had conceived, she looked on me with contempt. May the Lord judge between you and me!' But Abram said to Sarai, 'Behold, your servant is in your power; do to her as you please.' Then Sarai dealt harshly with her, and she fled from her"

(Genesis 16:4–6).

Understandably, Hagar was angry with Sarai because her insistence had resulted in a child outside of wedlock. Sarai now clearly regretted her decision and turned the blame on Hagar and Abram. Abram was wrong for sleeping with Hagar, but Sarai pushed for it. Sarai punished Hagar, but she may have been disappointed with herself, for she had impatiently forsaken God's will with her foolish plans. Sarai may have also been jealous that Hagar was pregnant.

After Hagar fled, an angel of the Lord affirming God saw her pain. He said God cared and knew that Sarai had mistreated Hagar. But because he knew of the plans, he instructed Hagar to return to the unpleasant, unjust environment.

"Trust in the Lord with all of thine heart and lean not unto thine own understanding. In all thy ways acknowledge him, and he shall direct thy path."

(Proverbs 3:5–6, King James Version).

I believe God sent Hagar back to Sarai and Abram because he wanted the couple to take responsibility for their actions. Sarai had to watch Abram love a child whom she did not give him, and God required Abram to be a father to the son he fathered. If Hagar hadn't gone back, she might not have survived, and Ishmael would have grown up without a father.

Hagar continued to serve Sarai (now Sarah) and Abram (now Abraham) until Sarah gave birth to Isaac. After Isaac's birth, Sarah, with God's approval, told Abraham to send Hagar away. This had to be painful yet liberating for Hagar. She left immediately, escaping the abusive environment into the desert where both she and her son, Ishmael, faced death from lack of water:

"And God heard the voice of the boy, and the angel of God called to Hagar from heaven and said to her, 'What troubles you, Hagar? Fear not, for God has heard the voice of the boy where he is."

(Genesis, 21:17).

The Lord provided for Hagar and her son so they wouldn't die, and Ishmael grew up in the Wilderness of Paran. Hagar eventually took a woman from Egypt to be Ishmael's wife. Hagar didn't choose to be Sarah's slave, sleep with Abraham, or give birth to Ishmael. God saw how they treated her, and He didn't condemn her because she was without blame.

After Hagar returned to Abraham and Sarah, her knowledge of God grew because she was aware of His majesty and power. Despite the pain that lingered in her heart, she gleaned great wisdom from her understanding of God. She used her experience to take a stand, moving on from the past and living in the present.

While things from the past can have an unhealthy hold on us, we must not forget how we overcome what happened as we might otherwise do ourselves and others a great disservice. The hurts, difficulties, and disappointments we've overcome will encourage others going through similar circumstances. By the grace of God, our examples will show the need to know it's not over until God says it's over. Hagar's story shows that there is life after sexual abuse, and it doesn't have to be filled with darkness and pain.

God will renew, refresh, and restore you. Remember that God's grace is enough for you. His power is made perfect in your weakness.

(2 Corinthians 12:9).

Snuggle in God's arms. When you are hurting, when you feel lonely, left out. Let Him cradle you, comfort you, reassure you of His all-sufficient power and love.[9]

CHAPTER 9

The Story of Bathsheba

"But the one who does not know and does things deserving punishment will be beaten with few blows. From everyone who has been given much, much will be demanded; and from the one who has been entrusted with much, much more will be asked"

(Luke 12:48, New International Version).

The story of King David and Bathsheba is truly one of the most scandalous stories in the Bible. In 2 Samuel 11, David made arguably the most detrimental mistakes of his kingship. He chose to stay home in Jerusalem when he should have gone to battle. This created the opportunity for him to meet and take advantage of Bathsheba, daughter of Eliam and the wife of Uriah:

"One night, he couldn't get to sleep and went for a stroll on the roof of the palace. As he looked out over the city, he noticed a woman of unusual beauty taking her evening bath. He was sent to find out who she was and was told that she was Bathsheba, the daughter of Eliam and the wife of Uriah. Then David sent for her, and when she came, he slept with her. (She had just completed the purification rites after menstruation.) Then she returned home. When she found that he had gotten her pregnant, she sent a message to inform him."

(2 Samuel 11:2–5, The Living Bible).

Bathsheba, painted as a temptress or seductress, is not accurate. Unlike David, she was where she was supposed to be, doing what she was supposed to be doing. The law required ritual washing after her menstrual period. A woman would be highly unlikely to conduct such a cleansing from her menstrual period as a come-on. If she were in public view, she would have washed without disrobing. There is no reason to assume that she was naked. Public nudity was not acceptable in this ancient Jewish culture but was considered shameful.[10]

David was entirely to blame, not Bathsheba. The king summoned her, and she could not refuse. Her husband, Uriah, was away at battle, and she may have thought David had news about him. David wanting to have sex with her was most likely the last thing on her mind. *"She did not know that [David] could stoop so low to trap and use her to satisfy his burning lusts."*[11]

However, David knew Bathsheba was a married woman. He felt he had every right to subdue. Since consent was impossible, given her vulnerable position, David raped her. Rape means to have sex against the will, without the consent of another—and she did not have the power to consent. Even if there was no physical struggle, even if she gave in to him, it was rape.[12] Just like Hagar, Bathsheba was in a position where her opinion didn't count. And without Uriah to defend her, it was her word against the king.

After David discovered Bathsheba was pregnant, he once again was concerned only for himself. He quickly arranged for Uriah to come back from battle, hoping that he would also sleep with Bathsheba so the child could then be passed off as Uriah's. However, Uriah was such a loyal and dedicated soldier that he refused to return home. Even after David got him drunk. In a final, desperate move, David murdered Uriah by having him placed at the front lines of battle. David then married Bathsheba, and she gave birth to his son.

David knew of the Ten Commandments, yet he deliberately ignored them. There is a clear-cut commandment declaring:

"You must not covet your neighbor's wife. You must not covet your neighbor's house or land, male or female servant, ox or donkey, or anything else that belongs to your neighbor."

(Deuteronomy 5:21, New Living Translation).

David's kingship did not mean he could escape the Ten Commandments and sin against God. David's sins against Bathsheba and Uriah didn't go unpunished by God. God sent Nathan the prophet to tell David the consequences of his actions:

"Why, then, have you despised the laws of God and done this horrible deed? For you have murdered Uriah and stolen his wife. Therefore, murder shall be a constant threat in your family from this time on because you have insulted me by taking Uriah's wife. I vow that because of what you have done, I will cause your household to rebel against you. I will give your wives to another man, and he will go to bed with them in public view. You did it secretly, but I will do this to you openly, in the sight of all Israel."

(2 Samuel 12:9–12, New Living Translation).

Because of David's sins, the child Bathsheba gave birth to died, but God blessed her with Solomon's birth. Later, David's son Amnon raped David's daughter Tamar. David's son Absalom then killed Amnon and attempted to destroy King David. He also seized control of Israel. (Absalom was the one who slept with David's wives in public view and got many of David's allies to turn against him in rebellion, although he wasn't successful.)

David's actions had dire consequences, but God protected and defended Bathsheba because she was not to blame for David's sins. Bathsheba became David's chief royal wife, and Solomon eventually became the heir to the throne, though he was not the eldest. He continued David's house that otherwise would have collapsed, and Bathsheba also received special mention in the genealogy of Jesus (Matthew 1:6–7).

Bathsheba's story is yet another testament to the nature of our God, who does not blame the victim but comes to their rescue and defense.

We can never be afraid to stand up for what is right, no matter what others say. And, sometimes, if that means taking a lonely road, if what we are standing for is true, then perhaps moonlight or sunshine will light our way and make it less lonely. [13]

Through these two women's stories, forced to have sex with powerful men, we discover that God vindicated the victims.

"For the Lord will vindicate his people and have compassion on his servants."

(Psalm 135:14).

There is a way out through the freedom we have in our Lord and Savior, Jesus Christ. He doesn't want us to be bound physically, mentally, emotionally, or spiritually. He will defend and rescue you. Whether you're currently in an abusive situation or looking to overcome a painful circumstance in your past, there is healing and freedom available for you.

"Honor and thanks be to the Lord, who carries our heavy loads day by day. He is the God Who saves us."

(Psalm 68:19, New Life Version).

CHAPTER 10

My Story: Honor the Value in Past Experiences

"I'm a mystery to myself, for I want to do what is right but end up doing what my moral instincts condemn. And if my behavior is not in line with my desire, my conscience still confirms the excellence of the law. And now I realize that it is no longer my true self doing it, but the unwelcome intruder of sin in my humanity … My lofty desires to do what is good are dashed when I do the things I want to avoid. So, if my behavior contradicts my desires to do good, I must conclude that it's not my true identity doing it, but the unwelcome intruder of sin hindering me from being who I really am."

(Romans 7:15–17, 19–20, The Passion Translation).

Having experienced sexual assault throughout my life; I can easily relate to Tamar and Bathsheba. Although my abusers were not all authority figures in the social sense, they were in my young mind. As adults, they qualified, and because of this, my soul became stuck in trauma for many years. Why? I did not know how to let go of the offenses, build healthy trust with others, or forgive myself to move on without feeling guilty. Because of this, faith leaders took advantage of me and spiritually abused me. This abuse left me struggling to open my heart and trust God because I viewed God as a man. Accepting a Holy Spirit within was exceedingly difficult for me to understand, let alone embrace.

I grew up in a cult-like, fire-and-brimstone-preaching church in Jamaica, and later joined the same denomination when I emigrated to the United States. Within this church setting, I witnessed the women in my family (divorced, widowed, or stay-at-home mothers and oppressed by men) obey derisive rules. Inadequately trained men in authority imposed these rules on them. The church operated under the guise of divine protection for women, including strict dressing guidelines and covering the head.

The dysfunction extended to the faith leaders, who dictated how and what female members should spend money on. Women had no voice and did not matter. Women were told how to comb their hair, what to read, how to dress, whom to marry, and what to eat. Women could not wear jewelry (except for a watch and sometimes a wedding band) and were forbidden to have short hair, wear makeup, go to the movie theater, date, participate in sports, or go to the beach. We had to seek permission to attend outside religious functions. There were many other human-made erroneous rules, and they expected us to obey them all.

I suffered my first abuse by clergy when I was ten, and they subjected me to emotional trauma when the clergy shamed me. While attending a faith-based convention with my mother, they provided me refreshments, and since I loved food, I ate a lot. My faith leader, a woman, noted that I didn't adhere to the etiquette. In her mind, I overate, so she verbally reprimanded and made a public spectacle of me. The church implemented a punishment referred to as "putting you in the back of the church." This shaming process involved making someone sit on the last bench so everyone would know that person had violated a human-made rule. The shamed victim was to remain in "church prison" until the faith leader released them. At this point, a public apology from the victim to the congregation was required. They shamed me under the veneer of faith and traditional religious practice, but I couldn't understand why I had to endure this form of punishment. What I found devastating is why no one protected me from harm or defended me.

To make matters worse, I had to remain in that environment where the traumatic experienced occurred for five years. From that day until thirty years later, they had crushed my ten-year-old soul. I remained stuck sitting on the last bench in the back of the church, shrouded in shame.

The spiritual abuse perpetrated by this faith leader stripped me of my fidelity to God. I silently and slowly attached my heart to shame and believed I was a letdown to my faith community. They left me distressed, disenchanted, downhearted, and tangled. This created the thread of skepticism to the point of melting my belief in God's sovereignty. Because of the unresolved feelings of abandonment, the sexual abuse, and the degradation placed on me for loving food, I became very overweight. At my heaviest, as a teenager, I was two hundred and seventy pounds. I hated my body, became needy, and began searching for love and acceptance in all the wrong places and from many people.

I moved to the United States at age fifteen. My dad relocated my siblings and me to the United States, leaving my mom behind in Jamaica. I thought relocation would be a relief—an escape from poverty and a gateway to paradise. But it was the beginning of more sorrow. Shortly after we arrived in the USA, my dad abandoned us again. I believed the men I loved would always leave me. With no parental supervision, we fended for ourselves. We ate breakfast and lunch at school and went without food many times. I was so deprived and was eagerly searching for the protection, acceptance, and love of a fatherly figure in my life. As soon as I was old enough to work, I found a job as a cashier at a local restaurant.

As a teenager, I was sexually immature and did not know how to handle all the attention I received from older men as my overweight figure made me look older than my actual age. When I was seventeen, I met my now ex-husband, a man twenty years older. I became pregnant at nineteen and dropped out of college to work and take care of our baby.

After the birth of my daughter, I fell into postpartum depression. I didn't know what was happening to me or my emotions. I knew I needed help and support to overcome my pain, so I did what I saw some Christian women in my family do. I turned to the church for help. My faith leader forced himself upon me, shattering my trust in others once again. This assault came during an already challenging time, and it wounded my soul, demolished my self-esteem, crippled my courage and faith in God.

At that moment, I felt like Hagar and Bathsheba. I was a woman taken advantage of by a man in power, and I felt destined to lead a sinful life. I went to the hospital, and the nurse suggested I report this assault to the police. But the leader who had assaulted me said no one would believe me, and I believed him because he was well-loved, and I saw him as a father figure. I was so low. My self-image and self-esteem shattered, and my faith in the world rocked.

My soul had become extremely toxic, corrupted, and sick. So, instead, I thought the attention and intimacy were the stairways to pure love divine. And I fell for it all—hook, line, and sinker. This faith leader took control of my mind. He made sure I included him in all my decision making. Whatever I did or wherever I went, he knew about it. I felt attended to like a little naïve, obedient girl. He had a deep need for excessive attention and admiration and a lack of empathy for others. He operated as a caring, spiritual father, ride-or-die friend, trusted counselor, and understanding life coach. His abusive nature showed itself in other ways.

The control was relentless. He attacked me verbally and publicly bullied me at church. He punished me emotionally, humiliated me, and created hostility between myself and others. He led me to believe that he did so out of love and protection, and he convinced me I didn't need anyone else, and no one would ever want me the way he did. Ultimately, he controlled me and every aspect of my life, blaming it on his ministry.

He started displaying stalking behavior, showed up at my job, and tracked me when I was out in public. I was physically and emotionally sick because of the stress and controlling treatment. I felt like I was losing my mind. Like a stone thrown into the sea, I sunk deeper and deeper into depression with no support to pull me out. I lost all hope for recovery. I tried to pray, and I cried out for God to answer my needs. I asked God to show me the way out of my suffering. He was silent. I couldn't hear His voice or see an answer to my prayers. I hid what I was going through from friends and family. I was alone. I had nothing and felt as if I had no one in the world whom I could trust.

I didn't know God had a destiny for my life. I had no idea what God had in store for me. I didn't know my value, my worth, or my purpose. I didn't know God could fulfill my longing and yearning for love. My life was in tatters, and with nowhere to turn, I could take no more. One day I drove my car to a bridge and attempted to drive it off. When I awoke, I discovered my suicide attempt failed. Thank God the effort to take my life failed because the life I longed to rid myself of was the very life God wanted me to have. Yet, I didn't realize that.

* * *

In my desperation to find peace and happiness, I turned to what we were taught to call "idolatry"—spiritual New Age practices that promised healing, love, higher self-esteem, and inner peace. I started following the law of attraction. This is a New Age practice that teaches that we can manifest whatever we want to and arrive at constant self-gratification and happiness.

At first, I thought this solved my problems. From my experience, this practice taught me that the universe is in charge of our lives and that I need not call on God because He isn't the source of our existence. I started accumulating scraps of desperation, hatred towards men, neediness for help, but instead of running to God, I strayed further from Him. I was angry with God. I hated the church. I couldn't understand why God didn't help me during my time of need. I struggled to understand how a man in a spiritual leadership role could be demonic. I had more questions than I did answers, and so I stopped believing in God and charged Him with the crime of the wrongdoing of others against me. That experience emptied my self-esteem and created a quilt scrap of anger, skepticism, numbness toward faith leaders, and an unwillingness to give my heart to the Lord.

I started thinking the "universe" was my source of support. I trusted the universe because I was not held accountable for it. I couldn't see it. I did not have to touch it or feel it. I could not see at the time that these false promises had led me astray and entangled my mind and emotions. But it always disappointed me.

Eventually, after years of trying to fix me, I realized that practicing the law-of-attraction was another avenue by which the Enemy leads us into the arms of evil. It is another avenue to isolate and control us. I also realized that this practice promotes living independent of God's guidance, love, and protection. I was never obligated or encouraged to talk about or rely on Jesus or even call God's name. It cuts us off from connecting with God, and it felt I was giving God a pass on His responsibility and his promises to take care of me. One of the most damaging things about this practice is that subtly, it felt I was being abused all over again. I think it teaches we call to ourselves the experiences we encounter. That practice made me the cause of the emotional, sexual, physical, and spiritual abuse I had experienced. It blamed me for what happened to me. When I realized what this practice had been doing to me, it devastated me.

One would think that after everything that I went through that I would run. But the devil used that soul tie as a stronghold to imprison me emotionally, break me down psychologically, and ultimately impede my life in a way I could never envisage. I was a gullible young woman who had fallen into a soul tie that almost choked me to death. I did not like the woman I'd become and was not proud of the girl I allowed that soul tie and traumatic experiences to create. I stewed in guilt, bitterness, and shame for a long time. I could not get out of bed for too many days, and I didn't know how to face the world. I struggled to find peace, and I felt like a failure because I allowed my past to stitch the tumultuous and tough childhood patterns into my present.

I didn't know what was happening to me until after I came across the famous Milgram Experiment into human behavior. This experiment showed how obedience to authority is ingrained in us by how we are brought up. Participants in this experiment went to extremes to follow orders given by an authority figure, even to the extent of seriously harming another human being.

It was then I realized staying stuck was greater than the pain of taking steps to change. I needed deliverance. I needed release and liberation from these feelings, and my sick soul wanted to heal from the perversion created through the soul tie. Intense therapy went some way to repairing the damage to my broken soul, and with Gods help, I could begin the process of letting go of patterns and whorls that these adversities left on my neurobiology

Opening my heart to help through clinical therapy that focused on helping adults overcome Adverse Childhood Experiences (ACEs) (The list of allies I enlisted to support me is discussed in Chapter 19.), I discovered a pattern in all of my relationships I had previously overlooked. I am a compassionate woman suffering from Toxic Hyper-Empathy Syndrome, a person with a high empathy level. This means I am empathetic of others to the point of mirroring the feelings and emotions of another person, and I feel things to the extreme. In other words, my excessive empathy completely prevented me from clearly seeing the predator in front of me. I was attracting relationships with individuals who controlled, belittled, and took advantage of me because of my high need to feel safe and protected. It was that little wounded girl that kept showing up because she needed to be healed, attended to, and care for. Therapy helped me develop skills to handle my inner child when she shows up, decreasing the need to want from others what I need to give to myself.

I struggled through the shame and grief of letting go of the soul tie. I realized my spirit was disconnected from God and my consciousness. But God helped and pulled me through the fragile process. He directed me to trusted allies who supported me during this torment. A nonprofit organization dedicated to helping victims overcome clergy abuse came to my rescue. I formed safe relationships and shared my experience without blame or fear of rejection. God gave me a community who understood my pain and my trauma and wanted to help me heal. I engaged in learning sessions, developing skills to make better decisions faster to experience fewer regrets.

I found refuge in individuals who reached out and offered to help me through mentorship. These individuals, along with my therapist and counselor, prayed with me, helped me face my demons, and walked me through the process of inviting the Holy Spirit into my life who encourage and empower me to reclaim my life. For the first time, I had people on my side who believed me and believed in me.

I got stronger and found the strength to remove myself from the faith-based community and confronted the faith leader who abused me based on the scriptures in Mathew 18:15-20. He refused to stop. So, I reported the incident to a higher authority within the church's structure, and they intervened. Although the process took a massive amount of time, self-courage forced me to forge a personal and authentic connection with God.

One of the greatest lessons I learned from this experience is how important it is to look back and see what you are doing, what lessons you've learned, and the patterns you've noticed. Looking back to examine the practices helped me get away from what felt routine, comfortable, and effortless. I was not arrogant of the woman I became while being during that dreadful chapter of my life. I fell, I cracked but owning the role I played in attracting and inviting toxic relationships forced me to seek support that helped me heal my soul. In the process, the light of God broke through my soul, illuminated my consciousness, and reprogrammed my mind to rethink my self-worth.

"Guide me in your truth and teach me, for you are God my Savior, and my hope is in you all day long."

(Psalm 25:5, New International Version).

My story reminds me of the adulteress's story in John 8:1– 11, where the religious leaders, whose motive was political entrapment, accused a woman who they claimed was caught in the act of adultery. Jesus silenced her accusers and instead extended forgiveness, love, and a chance for her to repent and become a new, transformed life within the body of Christ.

I love this story because the very men who accused her were the same ones God used to bring her into a personal encounter with Jesus. The religious leaders thought Jesus was going to condemn the adulteress, but it shocked them when He said,

"He who is without sin among you, let him throw a stone at her."

(John 8:7, New King James Version).

Jesus, the only one with the power to condemn, did not blame her, and He wasn't even angry about her sin. He saw beyond what she did and recognized why she did it. Jesus saw the entire context of her situation. This is a skill we would all benefit from employing before jumping in with judgmental opinions about someone else's actions or behavior. Instead, Jesus expressed compassion to her and told her to live her life free of sin. He showed grace and provided her with a fresh start and a passion for sewing a better tapestry for her life.

"Go and sin no more."

(John 8:11, New King James Version).

When I reached out to Jesus, He extended the same compassion to me. I chose to accept it and began the process of change, and as a result, I have never been the same. I had to confront the truth to stop the cycle of abuse in its tracks. But, like so many other victims, I was afraid to stand up for myself. Victims of abuse are often stressed and confused about their situation. This confusion can block the person's confidence to report the issue, or they ignore it, thinking it will go away in time. It doesn't.[14]

I knew that if I didn't confront the faith leader, I wouldn't be able to break free from the mental and emotional chains brought on by years of abuse. I've also learned that forgiveness is a system or a kind of tool we can use to release offenses, hurt, and anger. Repentance, like forgiveness, is the very air I breathe. Receiving and sharing forgiveness is how I've found freedom, happiness, and closeness with God, and so can you. You are a survivor. You can create, enjoy life, and be the woman God created you to be. In the end, you realize, as I did, no one is worth me poisoning my soul for the offense they inflicted on me. I want to be available for what God has in store for me next.

We have to stand up for what we believe in, even when we might not be popular for it. Honesty starts with being ourselves, authentic and true to who we are and what we believe in, and that may not always be popular, but it will always let you follow your dreams and heart. [15]

Healing hurts, it's painful, but then you are helped to heal.

Harvest

Gather the lessons
learned

...and DECIDE

on your gifts and rejoice.

CHAPTER 11

Your Story: Harvest

"I pray that the Father of glory, the God of our Lord Jesus Christ, would impart to you the riches of the Spirit of wisdom and the Spirit of revelation to know him through you deepening intimacy with him."

(Ephesians 1:17, The Passion Translation).

The stories you have read about highlight how those in power positions often take advantage of women. Being obedient, humble, meek, and afraid, Bathsheba submitted to David's authority and Hagar to Sarai's. These women may not have overtly believed that these people abused them, as they were 'told' they gave consent, but their souls would have known. When intimacy occurs due to a power differential, the lower-ranking position is usually the one abused.

Whatever his faith or belief system, a spiritual leader should take care of his sheep, not exploit them for self-gain or self-gratification. The sheer number of people abused by leaders has recently started coming to light. The tally is horrifying, and although this is a step toward addressing the problem, we still have a lot of work to do. Churches must encourage their attendees, whether children or adults, to speak up rather than listen to their abusers' warnings not to say anything.

Sexual abuse happens in the church, and it is especially detestable because no one in spiritual authority should use their power to take advantage of people. Abusive people gain and maintain power over their victim with controlling or coercive behavior and subject them to psychological, physical, sexual, or financial abuse.[16]

As you are rising to evolve beyond trauma,

Although your change will come with affliction, ridicule, resistance, and criticism know that when you place your faith, hope, and trust in God, He will clothe you with knowledge, strength, and dignity to laugh at the days to come

(Proverbs 31:25, New International Version).

Using the examples of Hagar and Bathsheba, I want to empower you to engage the Holy Spirit's help to become more aware of how others might limit you by defying biblical and even secular law. Become more attentive and fully awake to how authority figures abuse their authority and become aware if you are caving to them.

Change is a necessary part of life, and it will come with resistance. However, I want you to know that you must face and break every resistance that comes with change. To assist you in doing this, I invite you to explore **Step 2** to help you Harvest the mortification and guilt you might have felt in the past. Examine it, learn from it, and hold yourself accountable for taking steps to move forward. Remember, the Holy Spirit is there, ready, and willing, to help you identify the behaviors that support you in making better decisions. Based on the woman you say you want to be, use the list you created in **Step 1**. It is essential to stop and reflect on the steps you have taken to get you here and what you will do differently without blaming yourself or judging yourself.

* * *

H: **Harvest** and Heal Your Heart

Now that you know who you want to become, I want you to think about something that you are struggling with to get over. I invite you to go to Step two in your Thread Workbook. There you will find a chart with two columns and four lines aimed at helping you to look back, to examine and see what you're doing, what lessons you've learned, and the patterns you've noticed. This step is difficult because it's comfortable to stay where you are, it's routine, effortless versus taking intentional steps, and purposeful actions to change.

Ask Yourself:

- What lessons have I learned from the past about my decision making?
- Do I have a system or process I use to make decisions? Describe the steps you take to arrive at outcomes where you either feel stuck or feel proud at this moment.

- What knowledge gained can I use from my past to forge a new path forward?

Now write your responses.

Look Back: Crisis/Trauma: Name the situation you are struggling with to get over. E.*g., Being in a relationship with people who belittles me.*

Examine Your Patterns: Describe why this is a struggle for you. E.*g., I attract and invite toxic people into my life. I stay in these relationships longer than I should.*

State the Outcome/ Scrap: Identify the scrap. *I lose my sense of self-worth and dignity.*

As you're working through Step Two, I want you to speak to yourself as you would to a dear friend going through trauma. Be kind, caring, patient, and encouraging. Occasionally, stop, find a mirror, put your hand over your stomach, look yourself in the eyes, and repeat:

"I release anger, I release pain, I release defenselessness, and I will not allow the Enemy to weigh me down with what I wish I had done differently. I forgive myself and appreciate with humility the lessons these experiences were sent to teach me."

"To cause a shadow to disappear, you must shine a light on it." — *Shakti Gawain*

Now you know who you want to be, and you have identified past behavioral patterns. Be **tolerant with yourself** as you keep moving forward, and as you do, slowly shut the doors on any possibility of ever going back to the old experiences. **Your past does not equal your future.** Let's take those things you need to release, start, and continue and connect with God through prayer.

Remember, you are a work in progress!

* * *

In addition to the above to exercise, below are additional practices to consider as you work through step two:

Trust the Holy Spirit as the Spirit teaches your ear to discern that still, small voice. You will gain wisdom and strength to close the doors and walk away in dignity from everything that leads to places you can no longer live in, grow with, or learn from. You must release anything or anyone who takes away your freedom to live in true happiness and closeness with God, so you can walk the path that will lead you to dwell in divine peace, possibility, and purpose.

Own what you can without blame. Remember, it will challenge you to release some experiences, memories, and secrets you have been holding on to for years. Trust me, I understand. It may feel comfortable to hide them where it feels safe right now. But remember, what was done in darkness will expose itself in the light.

Spend some alone time in meditation so you can hear from God. What items on your list need to stay? Which one's must go? How will you build upon the ones you want to continue? One of the best things you can do is to be honest with yourself.

Honor the lessons learned. When life knocks you to the ground, gather the strength to use the stones you land on to build a foundation that will help you move forward with meaning.

Enjoy the abundance of goodness that a relationship in Christ offers. You are never too old to walk away from anything or anyone toxic. You are never too old to start over in life, to make the impact God created you to make.

Make a healthy decision today, a positive decision tomorrow, another empowering decision the next day; over time, what you do, say, and think will accumulate to make a difference for generations to come.

Practice saying no. If you still struggle with saying a healthy "no," discuss this in coaching or counseling. It is a behavior often interpreted as a weakness that can be open to exploitation by people who have dishonest intentions. Practice valuing yourself by adding confidence to your "yes" and by being comfortable saying a healthy "no," without attitude or explanation.

Remember, we teach and train people how to treat us. Do your best to protect yourself from anyone who might try to manipulate your trust by learning how to retrain yourself and others to treat you the way you want and deserve.

As you continue to assess and position the information in the columns where it fits best, keep asking yourself, Is this experience, event, or memory taking me to where I say I need to be, or is it keeping me stuck to the past? I've provided some supporting tools in The Thread Workbook to help guide this process.

A Pattern to Quilt – Harvest

Rise from behind your pain. Now you know who you want to be, what outcome you want to achieve, and identified some patterns that don't serve you. It's time for you to look at the threads you have woven as your story transforms. You see that the most important lessons are found in the process and the steps you've taken to get you to this point in your healing journey. Confusion and pain do not mean defeat. Give yourself loving attention as you heal. Learn how to speak kind and gentle words to yourself as though your life depends on it—because it really and truly does. Talk to yourself as you would another.

Remember, you're sewing a beautiful tapestry for your life. What you think about yourself, what you say about yourself, and what you do to yourself matters. You have come a long way. What's in front of you is better than what's behind you. Now allow the ease and flow of God's unconditional love to flow through your inner being. As you receive His unconditional love, begin to envision what the new you will look like.

"I forget all the past as I fasten my heart to the future instead."

(Philippians 3:13, The Passion Translation).

CHAPTER 12

A Prayer to Harvest

Father, thank You for bestowing the Holy Spirit within me so I can be powerful from within according to Your example. Lord, thank You for being the God of second chances.

Thank You for being a God who does not condemn but who is always willing to show us grace, mercy, compassion, and forgiveness.

Lord, please take everything out of me that is not pleasing to You and help me see what steps I need to take to prevent myself from making the poor decision I've made in my past.

Please help me continue to lean on your help to overcome the lasting effects of my trauma that have caused me to feel useless, hopeless, or worthless.

Lord, I believe that there is no situation too painful, shameful, or difficult for You to change. I pray You would create in me a clean heart and renew a right spirit within me.

Please forgive me for the mistakes I made as a result of not knowing and recognizing the truth.

You are the way, the truth, and the life.

Thank You for healing my heart and granting me Your peace today. I declare that my mind is renewed.

In Jesus' name. Amen.

A Time to Reflect on Your Harvest

....
....
....
....
....
....
....
....
....
....
....
....
....
....
....
....
....
....
....
....

....
....
....
....
....
....
....
....
....
....
....
....
....
....
....
....
....
....
....
....
....
....
....
....
....
....
....
....

SECTION 3

Step 3. - RELEASE

CHAPTER 13

Release the Trauma and Reclaim Your Life

"Let your eyes look straight ahead; fix your gaze directly before you. Give careful thought to the paths for your feet and be steadfast in your ways. Do not turn to the right or the left; keep your foot from evil."

(Proverbs 4:25-27, New International Version).

When you have suffered in a dissatisfying relationship, and at the hands of someone you love, it's difficult to surrender yourself and trust in future interactions. Letting go of being dismissed and unwanted is one of the hardest things to do because we are in a never-ending battle to trust that God fully is in control and has something better on the horizon. Maybe you struggle to let go of a relationship, hurt, past mistakes, guilt, regret, or worry? Perhaps you feel dissatisfied because no matter what you do or how much you give, it's never enough? Maybe you struggle with low self-esteem and a lack of self-worth because of an unpleasant experience in your past?

If you're experiencing these negative and limiting emotions, know that God can help you flourish despite the trials, tragedies, and traumas. What God has in store is never in the past or your fears or worries. God wants us to have healthy relationships, become more self-aware, know who you are, and move forward to see what He has in store. Many of us are patiently waiting, eagerly looking, continually dreaming, or desperately longing to experience relationships that make us feel adored, alive, comfortable, confident, secure, and safe. We search for honest, gentle, and kind people, and we would like a relationship that is easy, fun, and genuine.

As women, we want a man who will see us and accept us just as we are. We long for a partner who will stand by our side through sickness and in health, pray for us and with us. We yearn for someone who will help create fresh, new memories that our future selves will enjoy reflecting upon. Perhaps, like me, you may wonder, "Where is my King Ahasuerus or Boaz?"

To achieve this reality, we must first let go and RELEASE the trauma, allowing God to transform the bad into good. God can heal you to take control of your story. He can positively impact every aspect of your life. This extends to your children, your significant other or marriage partner, your church family, your place of employment, and your community. God is on the side of the wounded, and He will vindicate you. He will work for justice on your behalf.

In this chapter, we'll examine the Old Testament stories of two glorious women, Leah and Hannah, who transformed their pain into praise and prayer. God used those events to teach us:

Patience: Nothing that has happened to or against us has taken God by surprise.

Power: We don't have to allow unfair and unwarranted things in life to control us. Instead, when the pressures of life threaten you, press into God.

Purpose: You can flourish during tragedy and trauma because of Him. Peace is what we have in Christ.

Promise: God, who sees you in secret, will reward you openly. With His help, the things that typically have the power to defeat you will not destroy you.

"God will take what was meant for harm and weave it together for good. He will strengthen our hearts and hands to receive the blessings He has stored up for us."

Genesis 50:20

CHAPTER 14

The Story of Leah

"Though the mountains be shaken, and the hills be removed, yet my unfailing love for you will not be shaken, nor my convent of peace be removed,' says the Lord, who has compassion on you."

(Isaiah, 54.10).

It is natural for humans to desire love, affection, and protection from each other. Yet time and time again, we felt overlooked, unappreciated, or unloved in our relationships. In Genesis 29, where Leah's story begins, we find many lessons to learn as we discover the details of her life.

First, we meet Jacob, who met and fell in love with Rachel, whom he later discovered was his Uncle Laban's youngest daughter. Laban's elder daughter was Leah. Jacob lived and worked for Laban for some time, and Laban offered to compensate Jacob for his labor and asked him how he wanted to be paid.

"Since Jacob was in love with Rachel, he told her father, 'I'll work for you for seven years if you'll give me Rachel, your younger daughter, as my wife.' 'Agreed!' Laban replied. 'I'd rather give her to you than to anyone else. Stay and work with me'"

(Genesis 29:18–19, New Living Translation).

So, Jacob served Laban seven years to earn Rachel's hand in marriage, but when it came time for Laban to fulfill the agreement, he tricked Jacob: Instead of bringing Rachel to Jacob, he brought Leah.

"But that night, when it was dark, Laban took Leah to Jacob, and he slept with her. But when Jacob woke up in the morning—it was Leah!

'What have you done to me?' Jacob raged at Laban. 'I worked for seven years for Rachel! Why have you tricked me?'"

(Genesis 29:23–25, New Living Translation)

We know Jacob's reaction, but how did Leah feel? Did Laban even tell her about his deceitful arrangement? Maybe he also fooled Leah and Rachel. Perhaps Laban did not say to his daughters about his agreement with Jacob, and Leah assumed that, according to custom, she (as the older daughter) was to marry Jacob that night. Imagine Leah's shock and sadness when Jacob wakes up upset about having married her and reveals that he had been working seven years for her sister! [1]

"All who are oppressed may come to you as a shelter in the time of trouble, a perfect hiding place. May everyone who knows your mercy keep putting their trust in you, for they can count on you for help no matter what. O Lord, you will never, no, never, neglect those who come to you."

(Psalms 9:9–10, The Passion Translation).

Laban asked Jacob to wait seven days for Rachel, and a week later, Jacob married Rachel, his chosen bride. However, since he had already consummated his marriage with Leah, he remained married. This loveless marriage becomes a major source of problems, and it directly results from Laban's patriarchal scheming.[2]

Jacob is not the one at fault here, but Laban. While Jacob pursued his heart's desire, Leah became the disqualified wife he never loved or wanted. God took notice of Leah and was compassionate toward her:

"When the Lord saw that Leah was unloved, he enabled her to have children, but Rachel could not conceive."

(Genesis 29:31, New Living Translation).

God's love took center stage, and Leah conceived and bore Jacob four sons, and named each child according to her heart's expressions.

"She named him Reuben, for she said, 'The Lord has noticed my misery, and now my husband will love me.'

She soon became pregnant again and gave birth to another son. She named him Simeon, for she said, '

The Lord heard that I was unloved and has given me another son.' Then she became pregnant a third time and gave birth to another son. He was named Levi, for she said, '

Surely this time my husband will feel affection for me since I have given him three sons!'"

(Genesis 29:31–34, New Living Translation).

Blessed to bear Jacob not one but three sons, Leah remained hopeful that Jacob would love and accept her during the most vulnerable part of her life. Finally, she had a fourth son:

"She named him Judah, for she said, 'Now I will praise the Lord!' And then she stopped having children."

(Genesis 29:35, New Living Translation)

God's blessing on Leah did not change the reality of her situation, demonstrating you can be in the most beautiful and most painful season of your life at the same time. God can choose to anoint you to carry out an assignment and bless you with all the resources you need to fulfill His will, and you will still be unhappy with how His plan unfolds. Even though Jacob overlooked Leah and didn't change his heart toward her, God proved to Leah that His love and favor were more than enough. God knew Leah's mind was consumed with her feelings of abandonment and rejection. But she didn't realize that God had given her the honor of mothering Levi, the priest, and birthing Judah, the namesake of the tribe into which Jesus Christ would be born.

We often get caught up in the parts of our lives that seem not to be working out, and we fail to remind ourselves that God is working behind the scenes. God knew the plans He had for Leah and did not allow her to remain in despair.

"Wait for the Lord; Be strong and let your heart take courage; Yes, wait for the Lord."

(Psalm 27:14).

God knew Leah had praise inside of her, but it wasn't until Leah surrendered her all to God that He allowed her to give birth to Judah.

"The steps of the God-pursuing ones follow firmly in the footsteps of the Lord, and God delights in every step they take to follow him. If they stumble badly, they will still survive, for the Lord lifts them up with his hands."

(Psalms 37:23–24, The Passion Translation).

"Nothing that happens in our lives takes God by surprise. God is all-knowing, and He "works all things after the counsel of His will" (Ephesians 1:11).

He has a plan for each of our lives. Everything we're going through and will face He already knows about. Jesus says:

"In the world, you will have tribulation. But take heart; I have overcome the world."

(John 16:33).

Like many of us, Leah suffered due to her husband not loving her and watching her sister Rachel experience the happy marriage she wanted. Leah's desire to be loved and adored by Jacob drove her to find a solution, leaning into God. The truth is that sometimes, God uses our struggles to draw us closer to Him.

I admire Leah because after giving birth to her fourth child, she finally acknowledged the breadth and depth of God's love and grace for her. She rose to who she was and praised the Lord for how much He had blessed her. Something must have shifted in Leah. She took her eyes off what was breaking and crushing her spirit, and she started praising God, the One who had lifted her spirits. She started living to praise God, even though Jacob still didn't love her. When we live to praise God, He promises that in our mourning,

"He will give a crown of beauty for ashes, a joyous blessing instead of mourning, festive praise instead of despair. In their righteousness, they will be like great oaks that the Lord has planted for his glory."

(Isaiah 61:3, New Living Translation).

Leah stepped away from being a victim, quit working for a man's love, and propelled herself forward with a renewed mindset. She decided to praise her way through her pain. There is nothing more powerful than a changed attitude. To renew our minds, we must be intentional about the thoughts we focus on.

In Colossians 3:*2, Paul instructs us to set our minds on the things above instead of earthly things. I also love the famous words of David in Psalm 23:*

Psalm 23

"The Lord is my best friend and my shepherd.

I always have more than enough.

He offers a resting place for me in his luxurious love.

His tracks take me to an oasis of peace, the quiet brook of bliss.

That's where he restores and revives my life.

He opens before me pathways to God's pleasure and leads me along in his footsteps of righteousness so that I can bring honor to his name.

Lord, even when your path takes me through the valley of deepest darkness, fear will never conquer me, for you already have!

You remain close to me and lead me through it all the way. Your authority is my strength and my peace.

The comfort of your love takes away my fear.

I'll never be lonely, for you are near.

You become my delicious feast even when my enemies dare to fight.

You anoint me with the fragrance of your Holy Spirit; you give me all I can drink of you until my heart overflows.

So why would I fear the future?

For your goodness and love, pursue me all the days of my life.

Then afterward, when my life is through,

I'll return to your glorious presence to be forever with you!"

(Psalm 23, The Passion Translation).

"And after you have suffered a little while, the God of all grace, who has called you to his eternal glory in Christ, will himself restore, confirm, strengthen, and establish you."

(1 Peter 5:10).

As with Leah, God will align everything for you to receive your miracle. Instead of focusing on your problem, aim to gain, sustain, and enjoy the wonder. We must practice appreciating the marvels of God, even when we don't understand why we must endure attaining them.

"Weeping may last through the night, but joy comes with the morning."

(Psalm 30:5, New Living Translation).

Your tears are not forever, and neither are your troubles. Joy is coming in exchange for your pain. I encourage you to get up from your place of despair, discontent and head on over to the table God has prepared for you.

CHAPTER 15

The Story of Hannah

"And hope does not put us to shame, because God's love has been poured into our hearts through the Holy Spirit who has been given to us."

(Romans, 5:5).

Hannah's story is told in 1 Samuel 1. When men commonly had more than one wife, Hannah was one of Elkanah's wives, the other being Peninnah. Peninnah had children, but Hannah did not. Every year, families sacrificed to God to show gratitude to Him and to ensure His favor on their lives.

"Whenever the day came for Elkanah to sacrifice, he would give portions of the meat to his wife Peninnah and all her sons and daughters. But to Hannah, he gave a double portion because he loved her, and the Lord had closed her womb."

(1 Samuel 1:4–5, New International Version).

It was a great honor to be fruitful in the Bible, but even though Hannah had no children, Elkanah didn't discard or mistreat her. Unlike Jacob, he truly adored his wife and didn't want her to feel left out of the honorary sacrificial meal just because she didn't have children. However, Peninnah repeatedly taunted Hannah for not having children, making her feel inadequate, unworthy, and less of a woman—to where Hannah wept and refused to eat.

"Her husband Elkanah would say to her, 'Hannah, why are you weeping? Why don't you eat? Why are you, downhearted?

67

Don't I mean more to you than ten sons?"'

(1 Samuel 1:8, New International Version).

Even though Elkanah's love for Hannah was sincere and genuine, Peninnah's hurtful words poured salt into the open wounds of Hannah's insecurities. Hannah focused more on not having children and Peninnah's insults than she did on her husband's love for her, and more importantly, God's love for her.

It's important to note here that God closed Hannah's womb. She wasn't barren by chance. God's plan was for her not to give birth—yet. One thing we need to understand about God is that sometimes His blessings are delayed but not denied. If you're waiting on God to do something in your life, keep hoping, believing, and trusting that He will act on your behalf. Don't give up because it hasn't happened yet. You will not waste your waiting. Your miracle could be right around the corner! We can all follow Hannah's example of unwavering trust in God if we wait on Him and not give up.

"In her deep anguish, Hannah prayed to the Lord, weeping bitterly. And she made a vow, saying, 'Lord Almighty, if you will only look on your servant's misery and remember me, and not forget your servant but give her a son, then I will give him to the Lord for all the days of his life, and no razor will ever be used on his head'"

(1 Samuel 1:10–11, New International Version).

What I love most about Hannah is how she went to God and wasn't angry with Him. Even though God closed Hannah's womb, she went to Him in humility and with respect because she knew God was the only one who could change her situation.

If God has you in a waiting season, resenting Him will not bring the peace you desire. If you want to rise to the purpose God has placed on your life, you need God to help you push past the regret of yesterday and recognize you're still worthy of happiness and love. You don't have to suppress your emotions or feel as though you need to wait until you're perfect before you come to God. Hannah brought her anguish, grief, and distress to her Creator because she knew Him to be a problem solver. She knew her blessing was in His presence. She loved Elkanah, but she loved God more, as we all should. God gave her what Elkanah could not: the son she had been longing and praying for, as well as unconditional love, unspeakable joy, and everlasting peace.

As Hannah was praying, the priest Eli saw her, and she informed him that she had been praying out of her *"great anguish and grief"* (v. 16).

"Eli answered, 'Go in peace, and may the God of Israel grant you what you have asked of him.' She said, 'May your servant find favor in your eyes.' Then she went on her way and ate something, and her face was no longer downcast. Early the next morning, they arose and worshiped before the Lord and

then went back to their home at Ramah. Elkanah made love to his wife, Hannah, and the Lord remembered her. So, over time, Hannah became pregnant and gave birth to a son. She named him Samuel, saying, 'Because I asked the Lord for him'"

(1 Samuel 1: 17–20, New International Version).

Hannah found favor in God's eyes because she earnestly sought Him and promised to give back to God what He had given to her. It's time to give Him yourself, your needs, worries, possessions, and even your pain. He wants the good, the bad, and the ugly, so don't hold back. Can you still surrender to God even when you're going through a barren season in your life? Are you willing to trust Him with your past, present, and future?

Hannah fulfilled her promise to God by bringing Samuel to Eli to live in the Tabernacle of the Lord. She gave to the Lord the child whom she had deeply desired for so many years. She fulfilled her purpose to bring forth a mighty man of God. Samuel became a great prophet and priest. He later anointed David to become the king of Israel.

"I prayed for this child, and the Lord has granted me what I asked of him. So now I give him to the Lord. For his whole life, he will be given over to the Lord. And he worshiped the Lord there."

(1 Samuel 1:27–28, New International Version).

Hannah rose above her doubts, her insecurities, and Peninnah's tormenting insults and birthed her purpose. The Enemy used Peninnah to discourage Hannah from stopping her, putting faith in God. However, Hannah recognized her worth and knew that all things were possible with and through God. She didn't give up fulfilling her God-ordained purpose.

Hannah pursued God for what she wanted and never gave up on her dreams. Neither should we.

CHAPTER 16

My Story: Transform Pain into Purpose

"From my earliest youth, my enemies have persecuted me, but they have never defeated me. My back is covered with cuts as if a farmer had plowed long furrows. But the LORD is good; he has cut me free from the ropes of the ungodly."

(Psalm 129:2–4, New Living Translation).

Like Leah, I have an ocean-like capacity to share and receive unconditional love. However, I've always allowed that attribute to be the motivating force in my life, which has left me feeling disappointed and dissatisfied. Over time, I could not trust others, and I have pushed people away, a coping mechanism to prevent myself from being hurt. Thank goodness, this is no longer. After I finally formed a close relationship with God, I discovered people in my life loved me conditionally. It is the best that they could do. But God does better. God loves me unconditionally, and because of God's love, I didn't need to search any longer for love, validation, and acceptance. I simply needed to accept God's love and be the love I am.

As mentioned in Step 2, I was a teenager when I met my ex-husband, and in my early twenties, when we later got married. During that chapter in my life, I loathed the way I looked. I was hiding in a two-hundred-and-seventy-pound overweight body: a body that I used to cover the knotted, painful, and tangled threads in my life. In the beginning stages of our relationship, I grew quickly as a wife, mother, student, and business professional. Just like Leah, I tried everything in my power to win my husband's affection. I gave birth to three children. I worked full time and tried many things to create a happy, loving, and warm environment.

Still, deep in my soul, I was suffering from 'daddy wounds,' and because I didn't know how to process the hurt and pain in my heart, I did what many women do. I hoarded annoyance and bitterness. I lashed out in hurtful ways and rebelled for a long time, burying myself in work, school, children, church activities, and the wrong people. Like Alice in Wonderland, I searched, wandered away from home with my soul thirsting for love, fell down a rabbit hole, and was living as a total stranger. I felt so alone and disconnected from my husband. At my lowest point, in came the people - I thought they were super-heroes to the rescue.

Isn't it just like the Enemy to always show up on your worst day? You can imagine the inner chaos and confusion that clouded my mind. I wanted my husband's love, but the people coming into my life pulled me away by the strings of my insecurities. I thought they loved me. I felt they cared about me.

Like Leah, I was so focused on what I didn't have that I couldn't see what was right before me. I had a man who was not the cause of my old unhealed wounds, but someone who loved me the best way he knew how, and our beautiful children whom God had blessed me to conceive. I was still in the start, stop, continue phases of my healing journey, which seems like I was not making any progress. The quilt scrap I accumulated from my marriage was a deep sense of contempt for my marriage, defensiveness towards men of color, and disdain for the faith leader.

I felt like a failure because, like Hannah, I desperately longed for more, which prevented me from seeing how much God adored and loved me. What I thought I knew about God and His love was more intellectual versus a God experience. I didn't realize that the loneliness was because of being disconnected from God and my purpose. I couldn't see that only God could fulfill the love I was seeking. I didn't know that I needed to love myself first before anyone else could share their passion with me. I didn't realize that I couldn't give what I didn't have. I didn't trust that God loved me despite all the mistakes I had made. I didn't know God is a present help in our time of need, and all I had to do was to reach out to Him. The quilt scraps my damaged heart gathered led me to believe, once again, that I was unworthy, valueless, and not lovable.

I struggled to determine whether to stay or leave. I wanted to end the marriage, but I also wanted to stay and fight for our children's sake. I also feared the harsh judgment that would come from our family and friends. One day, I finally took off my mask and owned up to my wrongs, and our marriage ended.

I was desperate for a change. For the next five years, I started, stopped, tried again, and fell often. But I kept rising and moving towards learning how to receive and share forgiveness for past mistakes. It was not a simple process, yet the results were profound. I remember the day when a good friend who knew what I was going through introduced me to "The Ancient Paths," a spiritual healing tool by Craig Hill. This teaching centers on soliciting the Holy Spirit's help to break free from negative generational patterns and offers practical means in speaking God's heart of love and favor in our homes, marriages, and with our children. Craig Hill has dedicated his life to helping families to create and implement a blessing culture in their homes.

While attending a two-day "The Ancient Paths" workshop and later reading the book 'Forgiveness from the Heart' by Dr. Phillip Bonaparte, a beautiful breakthrough happened for me. During the first day's sessions, it led us into an exercise to release old wounds with repentance and forgiveness through prayers and affirmations. While going through the exercise, I saw my ten-year-old self sitting on the last bench in the church in Jamaica. The child lost after the public shaming, and there I was, looking incredibly sad and alone, waiting for an apology.

It took me back to that lonely time, where my life was hollow and where I felt out on a limb with no one to comfort me. In the workshop, I began crying with my eyes closed firmly shut. As I screamed at the top of my lungs, I remember the women in church circling as they rallied around, attempting to embrace me, and reach out to me. I shoved them off. I did not know how to allow them to comfort me. I ran from the church to my car and headed home. The facilitator later told me it appeared I was in deep mourning, having lost a loved one. I did not sleep much that night as my soul felt like it had gone through soul surgery. I was bleeding inside.

Somehow, I found the courage to return for day two of the workshop. This time I was quiet and no one bothered me. But I could feel the love, and it scared me to death. As I sat quietly on the very last seat in the church and listened to the facilitator, once again, I cried. This time my 20-year- old body lying on the ground, in the church office where the assault took place, 'met' me. As we came face-to-face, I could not contain myself. I fell to the ground, broken and knowing I needed help. Again, the women rallied around me as I cried uncontrollably. The realization that I had left pieces of my soul in those traumas hit home.

During my time of repentance, the Lord told me He knew I loved Him, but he knew I despised Christians "His body" because of the sins of my abusers. He showed me how far my heart was from Him, but He will repair it if I allowed Him to. It was hard. I was still stewing in bitterness, shame, and anger. I didn't know if I was ready to trust God. I was a pessimist. I felt my heart was fragile and did not know whether to dare to risk laying it bare. But I permitted myself and accepted His offer even with these emotions.

Following the Ancient Paths workshop experience, I embarked on a personal spiritual journey with Jesus, and he took my life in a spiritual direction. Below are some steps I've taken toward allowing God to help me end old, habitual thinking styles and behaviors that hindered me from living the life God meant for me.,

I established a personal relationship with Jesus. By getting to know God, I learned God was nothing like any man I had ever met. Especially not those who hurt me. When I was reluctant, God expressed kindness, extended unconditional love, and granted me patience and understanding. I had never met a man I could trust with my life. When scared, God would speak comforting and reassuring words that reminded me of His omniscient presence. He never condemned me. Instead, He, in the form of the Holy Spirit, compassionately encouraged me along the way.

I joined a local spirit-filled Bible-believing church and baptized. During this process, I learned to engage in conversations with God through prayer and found that when we spend time to pray and meditate, God opens up the opportunity for us, "His daughters," to approach Him as "Our Father." An intimate conversation with us on a personal level. You can tell God anything, anytime, in any language. Anywhere. We pray to get God's mind for direction and to understand and embrace and honor His will in our situations. I experienced an awakening, and for the first time in my life, I had a deep peace.

I relied more on the Holy Spirits' help to receive forgiveness to share forgiveness with others, and they would forgive me in return (see forgiveness affirmation on page 154). I wrote a letter to one of my abusers and asked them for forgiveness. Why? You might ask. I harbored hatred in my heart against them to the point could not love the people of God. I despised men. I scorned faith leaders, and I could not attend church for many years.

I am still growing in my faith walk and have repurposed my pain. I created *The Thread Movement t*o help women restore their faith, love, and life in Christ. Where survivors usually feel stuck, wounded, or ashamed, women can now feel free, healed, and whole as a beautiful daughter of God. Women are living a brand-new life as overcomers. They experience more joy; they live flourishing lives with no limitations on whom, how, and what they can become in God. They restore their faith, love, and life and are positively impacting the world.

I thank you, God, for making me so mysteriously complex! Everything you do is marvelously breathtaking. It simply amazes me to think about it! How thoroughly you know me, Lord!

(Psalm 139:14 TPT).

My Sister, I know you might say, like the Disciples in Luke 17: 5: "Lord, show us how to increase our faith." He will. Anger, disappointment, and blame had rooted deep into my heart, as it does when we are hurt and made to feel helpless. Here's the truth: Every negative emotion that we hold on to will become a distraction that consumes our hearts and keeps our focus from God. But there's so much power behind forgiveness. By cleaning out the past and preparing us for the future, God will rearrange your life and use what is meant for evil to help you cross the finish line to victory. Forgiveness allows us to return to a state of who we are, love.

I have been told of a Hawaiian doctor named Dr. Ihalekala Hew Len, who developed a method of forgiveness for healing: Self I-Dentity Through Ho'oponopono (SITH), which involves four practical steps to release the pain and contraction that lingers in an aching heart[3] - repentance, forgiveness, gratitude, and love. To do this, I imagine myself, or the person or situation I hold hostage in my heart, and quietly repeat:

I'm sorry.

Please forgive me.

Thank you.

I love you.

The hardest part about moving forward is letting go of what you must leave behind. No matter our current situation, God can transform our life experiences into something fresh, clean, and new. What's happened in my life has helped me connect to the love, power, and grace of God, and it has sharpened my desire to find and fulfill my purpose and help you find yours.

Release

What is holding you back
...and Recognise

...you're worthy of love, and forgivemess.

CHAPTER 17

Your Story. Release

"For the Lord, your God has arrived to live among you. He is a mighty Savior. He will give you victory. He will rejoice over you with great gladness; he will love you and not accuse you. Is that a joyous choir I hear? No, it is the Lord himself exulting over you in a happy song. I have gathered your wounded and taken away your reproach."

(Zephaniah 3:17, The Living Bible).

I don't know what struggles you've been through that may have left you feeling unworthy like Leah or hopeless like Hannah, but I know God cares about you. While the Enemy tries to torment you about your past behaviors or traumas, the Lord is showering you with love, mercy, and grace. He's more than powerful enough to stitch to perfection His purpose for your life.

Before we go any further, stop and check your mindset—take some time to think and answer yes or no to these questions.

- Am I taking steps to become the woman I say I want to be?
- Do I think good things about myself?
- Is there anything about me I need to change?
- Am I keeping my commitment to myself?

Consider exploring why or why not as you seek to answer the above question.

The way you answer these questions reflects your current mindset, and it is more powerful than you might think. Your mindset affects your attitude and behavior, which impacts your decisions and your overall destiny. Every action and decision first begin with a thought, which is why the mind is the Enemy's playground. If the Enemy can get you to have a negative opinion of yourself and a negative outlook on your life, your purpose, and your future in God, then you won't be able to walk in the fullness of who God has created you to be. The default setting of your mind should be positive instead of negative.

Leah changed her mind's default setting to see the truth that she was valued, loved, and favored by God. She found her identity in Him and His will for her life. One way to get the results you want is to control your mind and recognize your value. Before, Leah felt she had something to prove and struggled to gain Jacob's approval because he treated her as inferior to Rachel. This understandably triggered her insecurities. Leah sought her value from Jacob's acceptance and approval, so every time he rejected her, she devalued herself while overlooking the support she was getting from God. God blessed Leah with the fruit of her womb, but her identity was wrapped up in Jacob.

You are valuable to God. He fearfully and wonderfully created you in His likeness and image. God doesn't make junk, and He doesn't make mistakes. God has endowed us with gifts, talents, and features that make every person beautiful and authentic. Even down to the number of hairs on our heads, every person is unique. God created each of us as an incredible masterpiece, so our self-esteem should not be diminished because someone does not approve or validate us.

If you depend on others to define you or value you, you will lose your self-worth because of rejection and abandonment feelings. Sometimes God will allow the people closest to us to reject us and disapprove of our gifts and talents so we can realize that we don't need their love or acceptance to feel secure. God wants us to run, to seek, and stay close to Him, knowing that He loves us no matter what.

You have explored Steps One and Two in the previous sections; now, let's take a look at Step Three, Release the trauma, and reclaim your life. First, you will want to keep the list you created in step two handy as you work through Step 3.

You may feel unloved or unwanted because you never received validation from your family, marriage partner, parents, or friends. If that has been your experience, I invite you to consider disengaging from deferred hope and releasing the bitter and negative feelings, people, and emotions that do not serve you. Don't measure your value through the perspective of people who can't see you the way God sees you. You don't need to argue for your benefit or your worth. Let's examine a few ways you can guide your life to achieve the goal of releasing regrets.

R: **Release** the Trauma and Reclaim Your Life

T-H-R-E-A-D

I am so proud of the steps you have completed. Let's do a recap! You know who you want to become, you've harvested lessons learned, and I now invite you to **surrender willingly every unforgettable and unforgivable experience** to God. Cast your burdens on Jesus and acknowledge that what you have been through is no longer yours, and it now belongs to God.

Ask yourself:

- What do I need to let go of to become the woman I say I want to be?
- What are my top three values? (see values list in the Thread Workbook)
- Am I living in the highest expression of my values and integrity?

Now write your responses.

Go ahead and grab your Thread Workbook. Go to Step Three. There you will find **three columns labeled "Release," "Keep,"** and the other is **"Adopt."** Based on the "Lessons Learned" from the "Outcomes of your decisions" that you've identified and listed in step two. Below are three actions to consider:

1. **Release** corrupt information and unpleasant events stored in your mind. You need to "release" these as they contribute to your dysfunctional life.
2. **Keep** valuable information and lovely experiences you want to "keep." This helps navigate a way forward and inform decisions you need to make to transform your life. This is where the Holy Spirit comes in.
3. **Adopt** new experiences and fill up your life with the things that bring joy and peace from the inside out. As you invite that woman, you say you want to come into your home.

RELEASE

Go for a walk around your block. What things do you see? List them down in the column where they belong.

RELEASE

Let go of the things that do not support the life you say you want to live

KEEP

Keep the things that bring joy into your life

ADOPT

Invite in and continue along the things that support your healing journey

- Review the list to make sure everything is included in each column.

- When you're ready, close your eyes and envision Jesus standing beside you.

- Yield ownership and relinquish control over what you consider yours—the right to hold on to painful memories, the comfort in holding on to guilt, sorrow, and shame — to Jesus.

As you **acknowledge what you've suffered:** In your heart, I want you to believe that you deserve to live in true freedom from the tremendous amount of pain and trauma you have endured. Realize that you cannot change, edit, or erase your past, but you can acknowledge the objective truth about what you experienced. You may feel unsettled or concerned that you won't be believed. You may worry that others will blame you for the wrong done against you. Remember, it took courage for you to come through the trauma or crisis, and what happened to you was not your fault. You did nothing to deserve the trauma or crisis you endured. I know it hurts not to be protected, adored, and appreciated by someone whom you love immensely, but God will rescue you from your wounds of abandonment and wrap you in His loving arms. He longs to comfort, console, and cover you. You are an authentic creation of God, so don't discount your worth.

You can do this! All of heaven is cheering you on, and so am I as you surrender those things that left you feeling ashamed, guilty, and unworthy. Beloved, God wants you to cast your cares on Him; He wants you to let go of whatever has been holding you back from God's best for your life. After all, you cannot use the pain you've endured to manifest the healing you're longing for. Below is a quilt with examples of things I have released from my past. I have included an additional copy in the back for you to cut out the ones you most identify with.

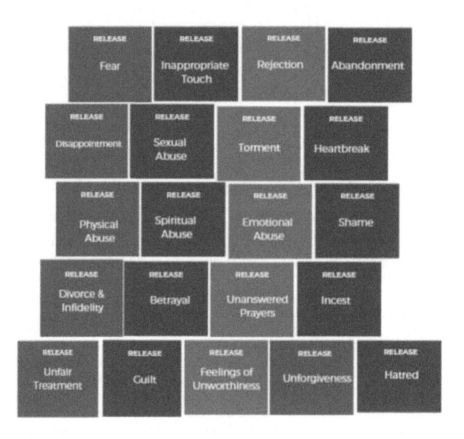

TAKE THEM TO JESUS

Below are examples of scraps or threads that you will need to take to Jesus as they have a way of secretly & negatively influencing your present. Feel free to cut and lay them down on the table in front of you.

RELEASE Fear	RELEASE Inappropriate Touch	RELEASE Rejection	RELEASE Abandonment
RELEASE Disappointment	RELEASE Sexual Abuse	RELEASE Torment	RELEASE Heartbreak
RELEASE Physical Abuse	RELEASE Spiritual Abuse	RELEASE Emotional Abuse	RELEASE Shame
RELEASE Divorce & Infidelity	RELEASE Betrayal	RELEASE Unanswered Prayers	RELEASE Incest
RELEASE Unfair Treatment	RELEASE Guilt	RELEASE Feelings of Unworthiness	RELEASE Unforgiveness	RELEASE Hatred

Here are my three" R" reminders to support your healing and as you endeavor to stay committed to becoming a better you. No rush. Feel free to try them when you are ready. As you do, feel encouraged, and smile because you're valuable to God. You might even tape these words onto your mirror or set it as a reminder on your phone.

Replace language that is passive or imprecise with positive, specific, and declarative language—the kind that shifts your thinking and makes you someone others want to be around. For example, when we're going through demanding situations, we often make negative statements like the one below:

"I can't do this. I don't know how this is going to work out. I'm so tired of dealing with."

Statements like these only make you feel worse about yourself and your situation and keep you from walking in the truth that this too shall pass. It's much easier said than done, depending on the circumstance in which you find yourself, but try to speak courageously and develop a mantra like the one below:

"I can do this. I can make it through this. I'm going to get through this. This is not my end. I am not fighting alone. God is on my side."

Remind your heart that you are valuable to God and have access to His peace that surpasses all understanding. He's not finished with you yet! Starting today, decide that you will throw your entire self into getting well. The key to growth is to learn to reject regret when you're not at fault. You are a Daughter of Christ, which means no matter how fragmented or flawed you feel, where you go to hide and bury your failures, hurt, and pain, what obstacles cross your path—Jesus loves you unconditionally. You have a loving Father forever, someone you can depend on to never leave you or forsake you.

Recognize that you're worthy of greater love, respect, and forgiveness, even when others don't give it. Let's not forget how far you've come. In step one, you declared who you want to become and the outcome you want to achieve. Go back to step one and remind yourself of the result you stated you wanted to achieve. Write it again in the space provided in this step. Be sure to maintain the inspired action you have taken by focusing on who you want to become.

In step two, you examined the things that no longer serve your highest good. Others' opinions no longer bound you. You are a Daughter of God who loves, cherishes, and treasures you. You can now make room and allow your faith to rise to help you uproot everything holding you back. Awaken the powerful woman inside of you by speaking victory to yourself and encouraging yourself in the Lord. See and honor how amazing you are because God created you that way! Try this as often as you can, especially when you first get up in the morning. Look in the mirror and say,

"This is the day that the Lord has made, and I will rejoice and be glad in it. I praise you, God, because I am fearfully and wonderfully made."

If you're ready to reject regret, recognize that you're worthy of love and forgiveness, and rise to the purpose God has for your life—pray this prayer with me.

A Pattern to Quilt – Release

The steps you took to release and reject regret took a lot out of you. Go ahead and rest a little as you allow God to renew your strength. Resting helps you to dream of a life-changing experience you wake up from bringing to pass.

Resting keeps hope alive, and it helps you learn how to trust God wholeheartedly as you fuel your heart with a new desire to remain committed to your healing journey as you deepen your faith and hope in Christ. Remember that the omniscient, omnipotent, and omnipresent God is for you, and He will remove the memories of past mistakes and give you power and strength.

Accept God's unconditional love, power, presence, and purpose, and rise above your past and quilt on, my sister, quilt on. And as you do, remember….

A Poem:

Your Life, Like Diamonds.

Your life is like diamonds,
Like the dark earthly matter.
Subjected to the purifying fire
That turns dark matter into crystals.

While you walk through difficulties,
God is there with you,
Walking you through the fire
Till you come out at the other end.

Shining and perfect, fit for His use,
radiating His glory,
drawing all men to Him.
Let the fire burn and be not afraid.
He who keeps you neither sleeps nor slumbers.
He cares for you still, Working all things for your good.

For every difficult situation,
Burns away your weaknesses,
Pruning, cutting, and shaping you
Into what God wants you to be.

Our lives are like diamonds
It is purified through fire.
Though life may hurt and burn us badly,
It brings out the best God wants for us

Chapter 18

A Prayer to Release

Father, I thank You for Your words of comfort and healing that have brought life to my situation today.
Thank You for reminding me I am loved, valued, accepted, and beautiful.
Thank You for giving me access to a love that will never leave me thirsty, a love that I didn't have to do anything to be worthy of.
God, I pray You help me see myself how You see me.
Please help me overcome the debilitating effects of my past that caused me to feel unworthy, unloved, and unwanted.
I know I am worthy because You deem me fit. I am loved and adored by You.
I surrender everything I have—my mind, heart, body, soul, and spirit. No longer will I live in regret for the things I endured that were no fault of my own.
I now recognize that I am worthy of greater love and forgiveness than I have received or accepted from others.
Please create a clean heart and renew a right spirit in me to rise to the purpose You have created for my life.
I thank You, you fearfully and wonderfully make me, and I will walk in the confidence and truth that I am a child of the Most High God.
This is a new beginning for me, and I will walk in newness.
No longer will I be a victim of my past defeats because I declare I am victorious.
In Jesus' name, Amen.

A Time to Reflect and Release

....
....
....
....
....
....
....
....
....
....
....
....
....
....
....
....
....
....
....
....

....

....

....

....

....

....

....

....

....

....

....

....

....

....

....

....

....

....

....

....

....

....

....

....

....

....

....

....

SECTION 4

Step 4. – ENLIST

CHAPTER 19

Enlist Allies to Support You

"These older women must train the younger women to love their husbands and their children, to live wisely and be pure, to work in their homes, to do good, and to be submissive to their husbands. Then they will not bring shame on the word of God."

(Titus 2:4–5, New Living Translation).

In this Step, we're going to explore the power of mentorship, which changed my healing trajectory, giving me a new perspective on my pain, ultimately helping me rise above it. A mentor is a real ally for you. Mentorship is a relationship in which a wiser, or more experienced confidant trains, guides, teaches, supports, and serves as a role model to their mentee. The dynamic helps the mentee overcome the challenges it presents them. The mentor will provide you with the necessary tools, guidance, wisdom, and knowledge to aid your growth.

Mentoring relationships are diverse. Career mentorships help the mentee establish and maintain alignment with their professional purpose and goals. Personal mentorship provides the mentee with someone to listen and offer advice to achieve personal growth and success. Spiritual mentorship is holistic as spiritual well-being is essential to physical, mental, and emotional stability. On the journey toward intentional transformation, a spiritual mentor helping to unleash your potential's highest expression is a godsend.

As we look at mentorship power and how to navigate the relationship, we'll begin with one of the most potent examples of spiritual mentorship in the Bible, the story of Naomi and Ruth. Many of us are familiar with this story. Still, the focus is often on the part about meeting our 'Boaz.' But if it were not for Naomi's caring and considerate mentorship,

Ruth would never have encountered Boaz. A mentor requires skills and qualities, and not everyone can be a successful mentor, as we will discuss later in the chapter.

Naomi showed us the ultimate example of a mentor who will help a mentee eliminate any of the remaining roadblocks that keep them from fulfilling their God-given destiny. A mentor's role is to lead by example, impart wisdom, and help their mentee improve in multiple aspects of life. For this reason, women should aspire to find a wonderful mentor. They should also consider giving back by becoming the kind of woman who can even learn mentorship skills one day. In other words, don't just accept the wisdom and knowledge. Pass it on.

"Iron sharpens iron, and one man sharpens another"

(Proverbs, 27:17).

When God is at the center of the relationship, the benefits of having a mentor are limitless. Humbling yourself and submitting to godly wisdom gives you someone else in your corner - someone to root for you and push for your success. We all need someone to lean on, so be proactive in reaching out for assistance.

"Give instruction to a wise man, and he will be still wiser; teach a righteous man, and he will increase in learning."

(Proverbs 9:9, New King James Version).

Even with God on our side, He encourages us to have friends to reach out to in person. As we study the mentoring relationship between Naomi and Ruth, you will see just how important it is to enlist trusted allies to help you mobilize your spiritual forces and take charge of your calling.

Chapter 20

The Story of Naomi and Ruth

Naomi and Ruth's bond began in the land of Moab. Naomi, the wife of Elimelech, was forced to move to Moab due to famine. Her family traveled with her.

"In the days when the judges ruled, there was a famine in the land. And a certain man of Bethlehem of Judah went to sojourn in the country of Moab, he, his wife, and his two sons."

(Ruth 1:1, Amplified Bible Classic Edition).

Naomi's son, Mahlon, met and married Ruth, while Naomi's other son, Chilion, married Orpah. Ruth was a native of Moab, and she was born and bred in the Moabites' ways, as was her sister-in-law, Orpah. As Moabites, Ruth, and Orpah served Moabite gods. However, as an Israelite, Naomi and her family believed in and served God. When Ruth married Mahlon, her thread intertwined with Naomi's, but they were yet to understand the fullness of what God was planning for them.

Upon Elimelech's death, Naomi was widowed, living in a foreign country with her two sons and their wives. Sadly, a few years after her husband passed away, both of her sons also died, leaving her with no grandchildren. Naomi returned to her home country of Judah.

Both Naomi's daughters-in-law remained loyal to her, and together they journeyed back to Judah. However, Naomi wanted them to be free to remarry and have children. So, she released them from their commitment to her, encouraging them to return home and find new husbands. Not without tears, Orpah stayed behind in Moab, but Ruth adamantly refused. She insisted on staying by Naomi's side:

Naomi's son, Mahlon, met and married Ruth, while Naomi's other son, Chilion, married Orpah. Ruth was a native of Moab, and she was born and bred in the Moabites' ways, as was her sister-in-law, Orpah. As Moabites, Ruth, and Orpah served false gods. However, as an Israelite, Naomi and her family believed in and served God. When Ruth married Mahlon, her thread intertwined with Naomi's, but they were yet to understand the fullness of what God was planning for them.

Upon Elimelech's death, Naomi was widowed, living in a foreign country with her two sons and their wives. Sadly, a few years after her husband passed away, both of her sons also died, leaving her with no grandchildren. Naomi returned to her home country of Judah.

Both Naomi's daughters-in-law remained loyal to her, and together they journeyed back to Judah. However, Naomi wanted them to be free to remarry and have children. So, she released them from their commitment to her, encouraging them to return home and find new husbands. Not without tears, Orpah stayed behind in Moab, but Ruth adamantly refused. She insisted on staying by Naomi's side:

> *"And Orpah kissed her mother-in-law, but Ruth clung to her*
>
> *. . . Ruth said, 'Do not urge me to leave you or to return from following you. For where you go, I will go, and where you lodge, I will lodge. Your people shall be my people, and your God my God. Where you die, I will die, and there will I be buried. May the Lord do so to me and more also if anything but death parts me from you.' And when Naomi saw that she was determined to go with her, she said no more."*
>
> *(Ruth 1:14, 16–18).*

Ruth's determination to remain with Naomi showed the unyielding love and loyalty she felt toward her mother-in-law, something that earned her favor with God. Although Naomi was not Ruth's biological mother, they had developed a close and loving relationship. Over time, Naomi had witnessed Ruth's devotion to God, and Ruth forsook her native land's gods to worship Naomi's God.

When Naomi and Ruth returned to Judah, Naomi didn't know God was preparing remarkable things for her future. She felt as though her life was over. But He blessed Naomi, acknowledging her faith had drawn Ruth to forge a committed relationship with God. Ruth didn't know that while she was in Moab using her 'helping threads' to comfort and care for her mother-in-law, the news of her kindness reached Judah. This whole time she had been grieving but put another first. The Bible promises that in due season we will reap if we do not give up (Galatians 6:9.)

Ruth did not know her 'helping thread' would transform her future to a brighter one. But, with Naomi's help, Ruth did four things that helped her to prepare herself for change:

She **listened** to instructions and incorporated the information into workable solutions.

She **adopted** new mindsets and behaviors, releasing beliefs and habits that did not fit into her life's latest chapter.

She **prepared** herself, so she was ready to thrive wherever she was going, and she was ready upon arrival.

She **worked** diligently, allowing God to open the door, exercising wisdom.

As it happened, Naomi and Ruth arrived in Judah during the harvest. Naomi used her mentoring thread to follow the harvesters into the field of one of her late husband's relatives, Boaz. Ruth determinedly gleaned grain for herself and Naomi from what the harvesters had missed, and Naomi encouraged her to do so. Being a foreigner in Judah, Ruth relied on Naomi's guidance and support to become used to Israelite customs and traditions.

While working in the field, Boaz noticed Ruth's undertaking and gave her permission to continue gleaning the fields behind the others who had harvested the crops. When Ruth asked why he was so kind to her, he replied,

"All that you have done for your mother-in-law since the death of your husband has been fully told to me, and how you left your father and mother and your native land and came to a people that you did not know before. The Lord repays you for what you have done, and a full reward is given to you by the Lord, the God of Israel, under whose wings you have come to take refuge!"

(Ruth 2:11–12).

Because of Naomi's mentorship, Ruth grew into a mature and humble woman of God. She had the confidence to walk boldly toward her God-given destiny, and she selflessly sacrificed her security. This filled Boaz with high regard for Ruth's decision to move to Judah and care for Naomi. Boaz instructed his harvesters to leave extra in the field for her to collect. In this, we see the principle of sowing and reaping in life. Because Ruth sowed kindness and loyalty into Naomi, who was the widow of one of Boaz's relatives, she acquired Boaz's goodness and favor in her life.

"When Ruth went back to work again, Boaz ordered his young men, 'Let her gather grain right among the sheaves without stopping her.'"

(Ruth 2:15, New Living Translation).

Ruth returned home and told Naomi about Boaz and everything that happened. Naomi advised Ruth, "stay close to the other young women gleaning in Boaz's field, so you will not be assaulted." Naomi cared very much for Ruth's well-being. She protected her in prayer and deed, not wanting her harmed. Naomi hoped for Ruth to marry someone like Boaz, who could take care of them and provide.

Under Jewish law, a "kinsman-redeemer" was the next-of-kin who married the childless widow of his relative. Although Boaz was not Elimelech's next-of-kin, he was in a leadership position. He could make positive change happen for Naomi and Ruth.

Ruth obeyed Naomi's counsel and ultimately married Boaz, becoming the owner of the very field she labored in. Soon after they were married, Ruth became pregnant and gave Boaz a son whom they named Obed. By listening to Naomi's wise counsel, Ruth found favor with Boaz, a generous man who also took care of Naomi.

When Obed was born, everyone rejoiced, not only with Ruth and Boaz but also with Naomi. Although not Obed's biological grandmother, she was the mother of Ruth's deceased first husband, so they considered her one of Obed's grandmothers.

"Then the women said to Naomi, 'Blessed be the Lord, who has not left you this day without a redeemer, and may his name be renowned in Israel! He shall be to you a restorer of life and a nourisher of your old age, for your daughter-in-law who loves you, who is more to you than seven sons, has given birth to him'"

(Ruth 4:14–15).

When undertaken correctly, mentorship blesses both the mentor and the mentee - it is not a one-sided relationship. We can learn much from Naomi's story, who is the epitome of bouncing back. Even though her husband and sons died, she became an ancestor of the most significant person ever to walk the earth. Our Lord and Savior, Jesus Christ. Naomi recovered from her distressing circumstances because she adhered to the following four concepts:

She put the comfort of others above her own. With a desire for others to achieve what she could not, she was brought to a new and improved place in life.

She offered unwavering love and support. Throughout their grief, she loved Ruth and Orpah to the point that they were willing to go on the journey with her.

She was courageous enough to rise from her place of sorrow. Together she and Ruth moved back to Naomi's homeland, overcoming roadblocks of grief and uncertainty.

She was generous as she guided Ruth in her leadership role. Naomi could easily have focused on her fears and troubles, but she poured into Ruth.

When negative things happen, God has a way of spinning them in our favor. You never know who heard about your trauma or who God is preparing and will use to help you on your healing journey. Naomi and Ruth had threads of loss, sorrow, grief, pain, childlessness, and widowhood, but God understood. He was compassionate in their suffering. He treats us the same way, empowering us to grieve and be intentional about caring for and feeding our souls. While in this process, we can discover the courage to deflect self-limiting beliefs.

Your loss is not the end of the journey. The T.H.R.E.A.D. technique helps you eliminate self-defeating feelings of sorrow. It enables you to see that God still has a purpose for you. We don't always understand how God weaves our thread into the beautiful masterpiece that He intends, but we can trust that He works everything together for our good.

God has further plans for you, so don't be discouraged by what looks and feels like loose threads scattered and shrewd. God has a way of aligning things when the time is right, and when you least expect it. Allow Him to be God in your life and present during your seemingly hopeless situation.

Everything that happens is a small part of our journey. We can choose to be passive, or be proactive, overcome our fears, set our own goals, and do our best to reach them. For better or for worse, we always have a choice.[1]

CHAPTER 21

My Story: Empowered to Make a Difference

"For I am the Lord your God, who takes hold of your right hand and says to you, Do not fear; I will help you."

(Isaiah 41:13, New International Version).

Thank God for blessing me with people like Naomi; overcoming and dealing with all the struggles buried in my past was possible. My mentors were the people who helped me thread my needle. I'm grateful for how they encouraged me, mentored me, and helped me believe that:

"I can do all things through Christ."

(Philippians 4:13),

and they taught me how to glean a harvest in my life.

After my divorce, I chose the shackles, bondage, and imprisonment set out by my culture, and I was not proud of the woman I became. I lived my life in shame and fear of what others thought of me. Like Naomi, I longed to change my name from Leonie (Leonie means lioness) to something I didn't feel as powerful and strong. I felt helpless, weak, and afraid.

Fortunately, just as God had other plans for Naomi, He also had other plans for me, as he does for you. My life, as it threaded through my healing journey, kept knocking me down with an illness, disappointment, hurt, and pain.

I tried, I fell, they broke me, but I kept getting back up because I knew that a battle is only lost when we have been knocked down and don't rise again. Rising from trauma takes courage. Don't give up!

Like Naomi, although I struggled with blaming, shaming, and complaining, I became intentional about getting well to overcome this. This was my number one priority.

One of the personal development tools that helped me seek my mentors was "Calling in the One—49 Days to Love" self-help book and an online program by Author and Family Marriage Therapist Katherine Woodrow Thomas. With this title, I expected to learn how to attract the love of my life in forty-nine days! To my surprise, the information assisted my healing of resentment toward the people who had disappointed, rejected, abandoned, and abused me. It was a tough 49 days, but, in the end, I could gather all of my leftover quilt scraps. I could place them in front of me, deal with them and free myself from the negative emotions and feelings of being taken advantage of by people who couldn't love me for who I am—a happy, confident, and beautiful Daughter of God.

I learned that forgiveness is the best medicine to heal a soul that's been crushed by the love it gives. In the end, we discover that love shares and bears. It gives and forgives.

I also accessed and used spiritual development tools such as 'The Ancient Path Workshop,' and I read books from authors such as Gary Chapman, Marshal Goldsmith, Joyce Meyers, and T.D. Jakes and I enjoyed transformational women conferences such as 'Woman Thou Art Loose.' Engaging these tools allowed God to do some deep surgery on my heart. For several years, I used the help of a clinical therapist, psychologist, coaching, and counselors.

Instead of continuing to be a victim of my past, I was eager to take the steps necessary to change my story. Enlisting allies to help me remove the mental roadblocks of my past, keeping me paralyzed, I finally mobilized the spiritual forces within me to stand in my truth and walk worthy of love and respect. It took me many years to love myself deeply and stop mourning the deferred hope in relationships that were not in alignment with God's will for my life.

With this knowledge, I was careful about who I chose to be my mentor because I wanted a confidant—someone in my life to stay, not take from me or leave me high and dry. There's nothing better than having a God-given confidant who will remain with you under any circumstance. Finding a godly mentor took time, patience, and prayer, and God blessed me with my Naomi's. These women have been an exemplary embodiment of the woman I wanted to become. As my role model, their life demonstrated the kind I aspired to lead.

I am truly blessed to have three wise female mentors in my life, and they are women I consider my wisdom sisters. They have been loyal to me in my valleys and on my mountaintops. They listen with patience and understanding, making me comfortable being transparent, vulnerable, and authentic to who I am. There's no need to pretend with them. It was the most liberating feeling I'd had. These women see beyond my painful ast to someone to love, genuinely support, and guide toward her purpose. They never made me feel less than the woman I was becoming.

My mentors helped me move toward becoming healthy in my mind, spirit, and soul. With heir help, I forged a relationship with the Lord in a new way. They didn't condemn me, but they encouraged me, fought with me, prayed with me, and supported my purpose. My mentors have taught me how to love God, love myself, and others. They've also helped me trust in God's plan for my life as I build closeness with Him. It is with this focus that I gave birth to my inner activist. And now, I am the big sister writing this book, developing tools and programs to advocate and help hurting women heal beyond their wounds. Now, I use everything my mentors have taught me, drawing on their patient and loving nature, when I mentor women. I have learned how to be non-judgmental and understanding, thanks to my mentors. Like Naomi and special people like each of my mentors, we are born to give life to another who is stuck. Our role is to help others who don't know how to move on. We can only accomplish this because of the hardships we have overcome. We need to realize God created everyone with and for a purpose. Part of that purpose is to sow into others' lives. This will result in us reaping the joy of knowing that we have helped another.

A few months ago, I received a sweet thank-you note from one of my mentees. She thought it hopeless to pursue her dream of studying at Harvard University due to financial hardship. Through mentorship, she received a scholarship and was accepted into the master's program at Harvard University. Hearing this good news from my mentee renewed my passion for my purpose. Here are some things mentees report because of our engagement. They:

- Launched careers that give them financial freedom and opportunities to impact the world positively.
- Are empowered to realize their potential, goals, and success in life because of the support and love they provide.
- Have achieved business and academic success because of finding their purpose in life.
- Have started their journey to healing old childhood wounds and have developed a greater sense of self-esteem and self-worth.
- Feel whole, at peace, happy, and complete as a Daughter of God.
- Are living a brand-new life as overcomers with no limitations on who, how, and what they can become in life.

"The Lord is good to those who wait for Him, to the soul who seeks Him."

(Lamentations 3:25, New King James Version).

Now that you've explored the benefits of having a Godly mentor, it's time to examine and start building your array of allies and mentors to contribute to your growth. Coaching, counseling, and therapy are meaningful ways to find partners to help you work through your past trauma, identify and heal your triggers, and find your voice. Prayer, fasting, workshops, and surrounding yourself with the right people according to your beliefs are fundamental to your spiritual growth and health. The most important thing to remember is that you need a community of like-minded people who will understand, promote, honor, and respect your transformation. They will keep you lifted in their words, prayers, and deeds.

Enlist

Allies to support and guide you on your journey.

...and Expand

SUPPORT CIRCLE

...your horizons and dream bigger than ever before!

CHAPTER 22

Your Story: Enlist

We should all be thankful for those people who rekindle the inner spirit.[2]

With the right information choosing a mentor is a straightforward process, and if you're seeking support to achieve specific personal and professional goals, you must keep these in mind. You will need to find a mentor who fits you and will help you discover the best version of yourself. Most importantly, they will value lifelong learning. To find a mentor and begin the journey toward intentional transformation, ask God to bless you with an expert mentor to create a rewarding experience as they guide you toward your purpose, not hinder you.

Pray and ask the Lord to show you this person who may already be in your life. It may be a family friend, co-worker, or personal friend. Your mentor should show constant love, care, appreciate you as their mentee, and show you how you can benefit from what they offer, making you hopeful, capable, and confident.

A good mentor inspires you to focus on your transformation, make positive changes in your life, and to continue to draw closer to God so you can reach your full potential in Christ. Mentorship is not about what the mentor wants, but what the mentee wants and needs. After you've identified your mentor, understand what to expect from them, and what they expect from you as a mentee.

E: Enlist Allies for Support

T-H-R-E-A-D

The heart of this chapter is all about finding and appreciating your real allies who will support you on your journey, and this is an exciting Step in your journey. Mentoring and coaching have helped many people achieve the transformation they seek, and these tools are incredibly beneficial. With them, it will not only transform you from your old way of life, but you will also grow into the person God wants you to be.

Pray for God to bless you with allies who understand you and who can help you thread your needle. These allies should not hinder you in any way but will build strong, lasting, and loving relationships with you that will change your life for the better. This is your journey. You can have a new beginning. If you want to reach a new place or form good habits, it is crucial to explore the available resources to break old habits. You want to be so engrossed in the new ones that you'll no longer desire the old ones. This is your transformation. Let's dive into ways we can *Enlist allies to support you.* You can't do it alone.

Yeaaaah…I'm so proud of you! Let's review the steps you've completed. You know who you want to be, you've harvested lessons learned, you've released fear, and now it's time for you to enlist allies.

Ask yourself:

- Who in my life can I enlist to support me?
- Do I need to have an impartial person to work with?
- Would I benefit from a coach or therapist to help me work through different challenges?
- What workshops or books will support my vision?

I invite you to grab your **Thread Workbook**.

Begin today by creating a list of people you want in your inner circle. People you've admired, who are happy, and model values and behaviors aligned with what you aspire to.

Include people on a successful path and whom you can learn from. Healing is a journey, not a sprint. Take it one step at a time.

Plan for what you want to accomplish. Do you need the motivation to date and marry the man of your dreams? End toxic relationships?

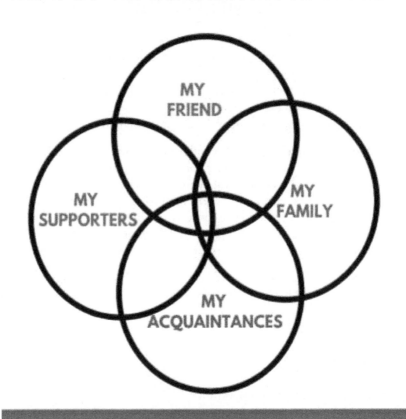

E: ENLIST

ENLIST ALLIES TO SUPPORT YOU

CHAPTER 23

A Prayer to Enlist Support

Lord, I thank You so much for allowing me to see the potential and the purpose that You have placed inside of me in the form of Your Holy Spirit. Thank you for opening my eyes to see that I do not have to walk this path alone. I pray You would bless me with the right allies and mentors to continue growing on my journey to a rewarding experience. I relinquish my past pain, guilt, and shame and focus on my future in You.

I stand and proclaim that I am worthy of love, joy, and peace, and I thank You for supplying every one of my needs. You are wonderful and worthy of all the glory, honor, and praise. Thank You for blessing me with real friends whom I can trust to assist me in being accountable for the new positive changes that I have made. I declare new beginnings.

In Jesus' name, Amen.

A Pattern to Quilt – Enlist

Right now, the needle is in your hand. Who and what do you want to become? Expand your horizons and dream big. Dream bigger than you've ever dreamed of before. Nothing is stopping you.

Maybe you want to start a business, write a book, go to college, get married, have children, buy a new car, buy a new house, or move across the country. Maybe you want to go on vacation or get a new job. Perhaps there are desires deep within your heart that you never thought were possible, but these are now bubbling up. Maybe you never allowed yourself to dream because you were always disappointed in yourself.

Permit yourself to live the life God dreamed for you. Don't be modest about your dreams and intentions because you can attain them, and you are worthy of all the love and blessings you can envision for yourself. Get excited about this new thread! The best is yet to come.

May the God of heaven …

Turn your dark scars into bright stars that shine so

others can find their way out.

Help you always to be mindful as God has a plan for your life.

Release new visions and dreams into your Spirit.

Enlarge your capacity to fulfill your God-ordained

purpose.

Activate your power within, aligning yourself to the woman who is healing.

Deliver you, so you enter the future, not holding onto or reacting to past wounds or hurt.

As you sew your beautiful new quilt, remember you don't have to do this alone. With God's help and by enlisting allies to contribute to your progress, roadblocks will move, and you will mobilize the spiritual forces within you. Bless and release the guilt and shame of your past. Become hungry for freedom, and repeatedly tell yourself, "The guilt and shame of my past are over." Amen to that.

A Time to Reflect and Enlist

....
....
....
....
....
....
....
....
....
....
....
....
....
....
....
....
....
....
....
....
....
....
....
....
....
....

SECTION 5

Step 5. – ADOPT

CHAPTER 24

Adopt New Mindsets and Behaviors

"Now that we know what we have—Jesus, this great High Priest with ready access to God—let's not let it slip through our fingers. We don't have a priest who is out of touch with our reality. He's been through weakness and testing, experienced it all—all but the sin.

So, let's walk right up to him and get what he is so ready to give. Take the mercy, accept the help."

(Hebrews 4: 14-16, The Message).

Have you ever experienced a crisis so consuming you lost sight of your true identity? This kind of trouble can destroy your self-worth and drive you to make poor decisions. Without even realizing what has happened, you become a person you don't recognize nor want to be.

Now that we've talked about the necessary tools to obtain intentional transformation, it's time for you to access and fully activate your faith in God and solidify a personal and close relationship with Jesus Christ. Trusting God to help you find the threads that connect your life lessons so you can rise to your God-given purpose depends on your having faith in God to fulfill His promises and mold you into the woman that He has called you to be.

You were born to complete a mission, yet so many situations will come your way that will make you feel flattened, and as though all you have left to move through life with are scraps. Perhaps you've wondered what to do with all your untold, painful, and even traumatic life experiences. In this chapter, you'll learn that by activating your faith in God's truth, leaning into, and depending on your relationship with Him to sustain you throughout every trial, you'll be able to come through anything life and the Enemy throw at you without buckling beneath the pressure.

Faith is defined as a firm belief or complete trust and confidence in someone or something. The Christian faith entirely depends on having faith in God's existence since we cannot physically see God. Faith is the foundation for your transformation.

"But without faith, it is impossible to please him: for he that cometh to God must believe that he is and that he is a rewarder of them that diligently seek him."

(Hebrews 11:6, King James Version).

Having a relationship with Jesus Christ begins with your belief with unfailing certainty that He is real and that He will bless you for seeking Him out.

In the New Testament, the English word *faith* is used to translate the Greek word *Pistis*. *The New Strong's Expanded Dictionary of Bible Words* says, "*Pistis* is the predominant idea of trust, confidence, assurance, and belief in God."[1] The Bible defines *Pistis* (faith) in Hebrews:

"Now faith is the substance [or assurance] of things hoped for, the evidence of things not seen."

(Hebrews 11:1, New King James Version).

Even though we can't see God, we trust He is real because we can see and feel His hand's positive results in our lives. Faith is directly connected to God. It initiates healing, translating our deepest secrets and sometimes indescribable thoughts and desires out of the spiritual realm and into the physical realm. Through faith, we can access every promise and benefit God has provided us in His Word.

Faith isn't pretending our problems don't exist, nor is it simply blind optimism. Faith points us beyond our problems to the hope we have in Christ.[2]

We cannot lead successful, meaningful, and transformed lives without faith. For example, if a woman aspires to become a lawyer, she must obtain the credentials before being considered a professional and officially practicing in that field. Likewise, as Christians, we must first develop our faith in God to exercise and apply His Word in our lives. By partnering with God through faith, we make room for Him to manifest incredible and seemingly impossible change in us, but first, we must believe. Faith comes before a prayer is answered, and it is our unwavering belief in the power of God to act that grants us what we have requested from God.

Faith draws us into an intimate and personal encounter with Jesus Christ, the

"Author and finisher of our faith" (Hebrews 12:2, New King James Version).

Through faith, we gain access to the heart of God, His Son Jesus, and we get to experience the true way of life in Him. Faith is also the bridge that allows us to cross over from doubt and fear into confident trust, which yields remarkable results for you and the lives you touch. Faith opens doors to endless possibilities, moves mountains, gives you courage and boldness, empowers your confidence, and enables you to achieve miracles.

In this chapter, we will look at the New Testament story of the woman with blood. The story shows an interweaving between the issues you and I have endured and the issues of this bleeding woman. The woman with the issue of blood was losing the very thing that she needed to survive. From this story, we are taught:

There's power in our words. We should speak positively to ourselves, for in doing so, we awaken our spirit and empower our courage to take the radical steps required to receive healing.

There's power in our faith. When we activate our faith, it will enable us to press our way through our naysayers' criticisms and harsh judgments.

There's power in our touch. When we reach out and touch Jesus through prayer, worship, fasting, and praise, He willingly attends to our needs.

Perhaps, like me, your trauma began when you were a youth, and it has been lingering into your adult life, causing you to lose sight of your identity in Christ. Maybe you've stopped believing the vision of the woman you were created to be. God can heal everything you have suffered and come through if you will allow Him access to the wounds. Your willingness to press beyond what others have placed upon you—what they said about you—will trail blaze a resurrection for the next generation of women. You are not a mistake. Say it with me, "I am not a mistake!".

CHAPTER 25

A Woman of Faith & Inspired Action

"If anyone says to this mountain, 'Go, throw yourself into the sea,' and does not doubt in their heart but believes that what they say will happen, it will be done for them."

(Mark 11:23, New International Version).

In the Old Testament book of Leviticus 15:25–27, Jewish law declared that a woman with a discharge beyond the time of her menstrual cycle was considered unclean. They declared everything she touched and anyone who touched her as unclean. The woman, with the issue of blood in Mark 5:9-25, was from Galilee, had suffered for twelve years with a continual discharge of blood that was slowly draining the life from her. She had spent all her money on countless physicians to find a solution but to no avail. Instead, her condition only worsened, swallowing up her identity and causing others to look at her with pity and scorn.

It must have been a lonely time for this ill woman, and they declared her unclean. Disconnected from her family, her people alienated her, and they forced her to separate herself from the rest of society. This woman had hit rock bottom. She decided her situation would no longer keep her stuck, and she refused to allow others to continue to force her to live beneath her purpose. Tired of her circumstances, she made the bold decision to reclaim her life once and for all. Her faith assured her she could, and would, one day recover.

When she heard Jesus was passing through her town, instead of remaining in a place of self-pity and mourning, she activated her faith. Although she was weak, something came alive within her. According to law, because of her condition, she was not allowed to touch Jesus, but she took inspired actions that changed her story's outcome. She pressed her way through the mental, physical, and emotional crowds that surrounded her. Crowds

111

of disappointment, unbelief, discouragement, unfulfilled dreams, forsaken hopes, delayed breakthroughs, negative mindsets, and people who had counted her out—to receive her healing and divine transformation. This woman had heard about Jesus, so she came up behind him through the crowd and touched his robe.

"If I can just touch his robe, I will be healed."

(Mark 5:27–28, New Living Translation).

Like this woman, we must abandon our negative thoughts and the lies of the Enemy and heed Paul's words:

"I'd say you'll do best by filling your minds and meditating on things true, noble, reputable, authentic, compelling, gracious— the best, not the worst; the beautiful, not the ugly; things to praise, not things to curse."

(Philippians 4:8, The Message).

The woman showed up with expectancy to where Jesus was, and because she was desperate for change, she acted. What tenacity! Instead of waiting for Jesus to touch her, she took inspired action, abandoned her old, hopeless mindset, activated her f a i t h , and reached out. She was low, so she touched the lowest and dustiest part of His robe. But Jesus met her right where she was:

"Immediately, the bleeding stopped, and she could feel in her body that she had been healed of her terrible condition. Jesus realized at once that healing power had gone out from him, so he turned around in the crowd and asked, 'Who touched my robe?' His disciples said to him, 'Look at this crowd pressing around you. How can you ask, "Who touched me?"' But he kept on looking around to see who had done it."

(Mark 5:29–32, New Living Translation).

As a daughter of God, you have permission to use the power of your faith to bring things out of the supernatural and into the natural. You do not need anyone's permission to activate or to use your faith. Don't let your past hurts and disappointments cause you to forsake your faith. You need your faith to succeed in your pursuit of health and wellness. Don't apologize for seeking prosperity and health. Rise, breakthrough self-doubt, and possess your right to your health. From this day forward, know that your faith has the power to make you whole.

Your faith will shift the way you approach the restoration and recovery of your health. Do you know stress causes many of the sicknesses we experience? How about taking the same energy you put toward stress and using it to fuel your faith? Turn your complaining into the expectation that something good is going to happen. Pray and give thanks to God for the opportunity to grow your faith. Ask Him for clarity and peace in whatever you face, and know that He is faithful to supply the answer or peace you need.

"Then the frightened woman, trembling at the realization of what had happened to her, came and fell to her knees in front of [Jesus] and told him what she had done. And he said to her, 'Daughter, your faith has made you well. Go in peace. Your suffering is over'"

(Mark 5:33–34, New Living Translation).

The life and authority of Jesus superseded every law and precedent established in the Old Testament. Through the power of Jesus Christ, every curse and a shred of condemnation associated with the Old Testament laws could be abolished.

This serves as a great reminder that a limited vision, self-defeating behavior, and negative speaking and thinking locks up your faith. You must stir up and use the gift of faith that God has given you. Show God that you're ready for a change to happen. Faith is active; it expects and hopes for the best, keeps you believing even when there are no signs, and propels you forward with positive momentum.

CHAPTER 26

My Story. Living by Faith

You may not control all the events that happen to you, but you can decide not to be reduced by them.[3.] I can identify with the woman with the issue of blood because I healed from two illnesses that attacked my brain and threatened my mobility.

First, I developed Bell's palsy at the age of twenty-three. I had just finished celebrating the news that I was pregnant with our second child. At work, I tucked into a huge Jamaican dish for lunch and enjoyed a few cherries for dessert. As I ate the cherries, they started sliding from one side of my mouth. It felt as though I was losing my sense of taste, as my tongue numbed. In a matter of seconds, my mouth no longer felt part of my face.

As an optimist, I concluded it was likely a food allergy. Still, I was afraid whatever was happening could negatively affect the baby, so I left work early and called my doctor. By this point, I was reeling with mouth pain, struggling to make myself understood, my words slurring. He told me to come for an examination. On my way there, my left eye became sensitive, watery, and painful. I struggled to close it and thought maybe I was crying but didn't realize it. I tried to drink water but couldn't hold the straw in my mouth. A glance in the mirror showed my lips sagged on the left side, and I couldn't smile. It finally hit me. I had no movement on that side of my face, and I cried. This must be a stroke?

My doctor diagnosed me with I Bell's palsy and advised me what to expect throughout the pregnancy and potentially afterward. I immediately blamed myself for something that couldn't possibly have been my fault. My eyes, face, and speech progressively deteriorated. I cried myself to sleep and took a few days off work to stay home, buried in shame. I couldn't completely close my eyes, and my tongue, lips, and face hurt so much that I couldn't fully smile either. Drinking from a cup without spilling the liquid was difficult, and I drooled profusely. I wanted to express my feelings but found it hard to translate my thoughts into sensible speech. I felt as though I had lost control, and Bell's palsy, a thief of destiny, took over every part of my face, speech, and mind.

For the next nine months, I pulled up quilt scraps of shame, guilt, and unworthiness. I felt ugly and miserable. I covered my mouth when I spoke to anyone. I also developed migraines and severe pain in the back of my head amid the ongoing facial pain. I felt lonely, helpless, confused, sad, and worried that something might happen to my child, so I carried a deep sense of fear and anxiety for several months.

My confidence hit rock bottom, and I walked around in shame because of my appearance. I isolated myself to avoid the stares and questions and grew more depressed because of overly opinionated people's hostile looks and comments. At the church where I worshiped, a woman told me that God punishes me for my unconfessed sins. I believed her, and hearing this negative comment crippled my hope for any recovery.

Thankfully, it was a temporary affliction.

One day, while I was walking with my older daughter, our landlady, a medical doctor, saw me and reached out. She knew right away that I had Bell's palsy and offered me the best advice to recover from the illness, which was to practice self-care and believe all would be well. I've provided a list of self-care ideas (see page 215) for you to consider. Bell's palsy had taken me hostage, mentally, physically, and emotionally. But her words were a ray of hope. I struggled with the illness for my entire pregnancy, but I lived my life the best I knew how.

Encourage yourself, believe in yourself, and love yourself. Never doubt who you are.[4] While I was waiting for my symptoms to diminish, God showed me several strategies to overcome the stronghold Bell's palsy had on me. I implemented different natural remedies, including meditation, gentle facial massages, and taking prenatal vitamin supplements for my health and the baby's nerve growth, all of which helped quicken the recovery of my damaged facial nerves. I also went to therapy and counseling to help with my mental and spiritual well-being.

Besides these remedies and resources, other things had a positive impact on my recovery. I encourage you to try them too:

Encourage yourself: You've survived whatever you were faced with. Acknowledging this is enough - celebrate your efforts and the progress you've made.

Treat yourself and speak to yourself the way you would a good friend. Encourage yourself to use the Word of God.

Smile: A real smile can quickly and naturally lift your spirits. It's like you're showing no fear and that despite your circumstances, you'll be happy because you have Jesus on your side. Smiling also contributes to longevity, as it helps increase your well-being and general happiness. Smiling makes you more likable and courteous, which yields lovely results for yourself and others.[5]

Laugh: While smiling boosts your happiness, laughing is a physical manifestation that your situation does not perturb you because you know the one called "Abba Father." Like Sarah, with laughter, you can boldly say God has your back.

"God has made laughter for me; everyone who hears will laugh with me."

(Genesis 21:6, ESV).

Some of the simple ways I brought laughter back into my life was to watch funny shows and movies, listen to some comedy, read jokes and quotes of the day. I also read funny children's books while spending time with my daughter.

Play: Dwelling on your present situation will keep you feeling sad, worried, and stressed, but tapping into your inner child can take your mind off your troubles. A friend encouraged me to volunteer in the toddler classroom at the preschool where I worked, which was a breakthrough in my healing process. One child asked if I was now the class clown. I said yes, and every afternoon I changed out of my work clothes into a red clown suit and allowed twenty toddlers the joy of my crooked smile for thirty minutes. It was painful for me to flex my facial muscles, but seeing these innocent children take pleasure in something I thought was so painful made me smile from the inside out. For the first time, I noticed that something good could come from my pain.

Coloring: Creativity is a powerful way to craft new and beautiful things, so even when your situation feels out of your control, harnessing your creativity gives you the power to make something wonderful. Coloring, painting, sewing, making crafts, and writing are all ways to create something you can be proud of, and it allows you to remember even when life is difficult, there are joy and happiness to be found. I also developed a passion for coloring during my recovery and have created a coloring book with twenty-one designs as part of The Thread collection. Coloring is not just for kids; there are some beautiful adult coloring books out there that reduce stress and anxiety.

Eat well and rest: Unless when fasting, it's not recommended that we go without food. Situations can make us lose our appetite but eating healthy food gives us the physical strength to fight. In the Bible, Paul suggested this to the people on a ship with him when they were afraid:

"Therefore, I urge you to take some food. For it will give you strength, for not a hair is to perish from the head of any of you."

(Acts, 27:34).

Besides feeding the body with the right foods, we must carve out meaningful time to exercise and rest, one of the best ways to rejuvenate and restore a well-fed body. In doing so, the seed of healing took root in my heart, and it restored strength to my face. I was smiling again, and I have been smiling ever since.

Give: Giving when you feel ready and in your unique way can bring you inner joy and fulfillment. Blessing others helped me see it wasn't all about me. I started writing short, inspirational messages and texted them daily to my girlfriends, encouraging them to build their faith in God; in doing so, I was also inspired. As I did this, God, through His Holy Spirit, kept whispering into my spirit promises so grand that my faith grew as tall as a mountain.

Practice self-care: Self-care is not selfish; it is a vital part of the healing process. It can be as simple as a warm bath or as extravagant as going to the spa. Take some time to focus on loving and nurturing yourself. Daily, I would affirm, "I now release with joy every sickness, every disease, every pain, and every misaligned emotion from my body. I bless with love my being and welcome with joy my well-being. My body is healed, and I appreciate my body parts for their support in helping me to fulfill my purpose." I still do that today. Love and appreciate the body God has blessed you with.

Forgive: Forgiving yourself, and others give you a peace not found in physical possessions or activities. Because I blamed myself for Bell's palsy, I had to release the blame and regret, knowing that it wasn't my fault. I also had to forgive everyone who had looked down on and talked about me because of my condition. Release the negative emotions and the burden that comes from carrying them.

Embrace Peace: It doesn't matter how loud the surrounding noise is. Make sure it's not noisier inside of you. Watch over your heart, for from it flows the source of life (Proverbs 4:23). Protect the personal peace of your heart, for, in the absence of peace, turmoil abounds. "And the peace of God, which surpasses all understanding, will guard your hearts and your minds in Christ Jesus" (Philippians 4:7). Let His peace wash over you, cleansing away your doubt, fear, and anxiety.

Activate your faith: Until that walk with my daughter, I spent many days in isolation and hopelessness. I began praying, reading, reciting God's Word, and giving thanks, activating my faith in God's power to heal me of this illness, just like the woman with the issue of blood. Jeremiah 17:14 became one of my favorite prayers:

"Heal me, Lord, and I will be healed; save me, and I will be saved, for you are the one I praise."

(Jeremiah 17:14, New International Version).

This Scripture motivated me to wake up daily with the expectancy that I would heal. I also read, sang, and meditated on this Scripture:

"This is what I want you to do: Ask the Father for whatever is in keeping with the things I've revealed to you. Ask in my name, according to my will, and he'll most certainly give it to you. Your joy will be a river overflowing its banks!"

(John 16:23–24, The Message).

During my battle with Bell's palsy, God blessed me with the resources to purchase my first home, and I pressed my way through college and completed my bachelor's degree. The paralysis in my face went away shortly after I gave birth to my daughter. However, it took several months to regain full health and feel like me again. Thank God for all the support and resources He provided for me; they brought healing in my life sooner than I expected.

"And I will bring your health back and heal your wounds," says the Lord, "because other people said you were outcasts. They said, 'No one cares about Zion.'"

(Jeremiah 30:17, Easy to Read).

God is a rewarder of those who diligently seek Him, and He will not make us ashamed for trusting in Him. My faith didn't remove the pain, but it got me through the pain. Trusting God didn't diminish or vanquish the anguish, but it enabled me to endure it.[6]

* * *

About ten years after my recovery from Bell's palsy, I was offered a new employment position in another state. This change of fate focused me on moving on from my divorce, raising my girls, finishing my doctorate, and starting a new chapter in our lives by relocating to the west coast. Leaving everything and everyone behind on the East Coast made me feel I had let down everyone I loved. I felt more alone and helpless than ever before. To make matters worse, I lived in a new city, had started a new job, had no friends, did not know whom to trust, had no one close by to reach out to, all while raising three children as a single mother.

My new job was incredibly stressful, and with all of my responsibilities, I was feeling spiritual, mentally, and physically exhausted. My body could only take so much, and I spiraled into a deep depression that culminated in a stroke at the age of thirty-six. I had thought only older people had strokes. Not so! While at work, I started with a severe migraine. Numbness encompassed the right side of my body like someone had poured freezing-cold water on me. My face was in pain, my body was weak, and I thought I was experiencing the flu or another Bell's palsy attack. My brain felt strangely twisted, like a pretzel being formed.

Despite the symptoms, it didn't occur to me; I was having a stroke. Somehow, I drove myself home. And I genuinely believe it was an angel of the Lord who took the wheel and drove me home by the grace of God because I couldn't move when I arrived. My daughters helped me from the car and into the house. As I fell into bed, I remained convinced this was probably Bell's palsy.

The next morning, I called a friend who was a medical doctor and explained to him what was going on in my body. He advised me to see a doctor immediately, but I stayed home in bed. I was sad, and the pain only worsened. I blamed myself for another health failure

118

and feared what my family would say and think of me. I told myself that after all the effort to start over and provide a better life for my children, I wouldn't even be able to take care of them.

While going through these difficulties, I couldn't see that things would get better someday. I lived under a massive cloud of hopelessness. I mustered up the courage to go to urgent care a couple of days later, and the doctor confirmed I had suffered more than one minor stroke. I was so confused about why this was happening to me now when I tried to get my new life in order. I continued to self-blame and told myself that God was punishing me.

As I embarked on another healing journey, getting well scared me. I had become accustomed to being the woman who was crippled and comfortable with the familiar feeling of being unwell. I self-sabotaged and told myself that if I took time to heal, someone might try to harm me like my cousin did while recovering from bronchitis as a child. That story made me feel safe, and it was soothing. However, it didn't help me recover; instead, it rendered me stuck. Over time, I learned how debilitating this mindset was and that I needed to rely on God's strength to stand again.

Because of the severity of the traumatic injuries I battled over the years, I knew I must build a safe support system to heal my emotional wounds. It took an army of diverse people from all over the world to help me improve my fine-motor skills, restore my cognitive functioning. Along the healing journey, I learned how to manage and cope with symptoms of posttraumatic stress disorder, develop self-esteem and overall emotional, physical, and mental well-being, and get rid of toxic, unhealthy behaviors and friends. Over time, I created a powerful circle of family and friends. The following resources also helped me heal from the stroke and my past:

Therapy: I went through intense therapy to learn how to think for myself, remember things, read, talk properly, hold items in my hands, and walk again. It took several months before I could use my right side again, but I worked at it every day until my movement normalized.

Online Prayer Group: I joined an online Christian prayer and Bible study group where hundreds of callers worldwide participate daily to share the Word, pray for one another, and encourage each other. This prayer team took care of me spiritually and introduced me to the 21-Day Daniel Fast. Daniel, an Old Testament prophet, goes on a diet where he eats only vegetables and water for ten days. After the twenty-one-day fast to gain control of my eating, I changed my diet for good. I eliminated sugar and salt in my diet and started drinking more water and walking every day while reading as much as possible and ending toxic relationships.

My Dog, J'Lala: I adopted my dog from an animal shelter after being abandoned by her owner. My J-Lala has become my cuddle buddy and the best welcoming committee anyone could ask for. She also encourages me to get out, run, and play with her, which helped me relearn how to throw a ball.

My Children: My children are the thread that pulled me up to rise above the effects of the stroke so I could be there for them the way I wanted to be. Because I am the sole provider in my home, I remained determined to get better for my children.

Coaching: I sought a professional executive coach and went into this coaching engagement with an open mind and a real willingness to uncover the problem, adjust my actions, and modify my behaviors for increasingly positive results. Cindy W. utilized an "Energy Leadership" tool that helped me understand my strengths, embrace my weaknesses, and discover how to see myself with "fair witness" eyes and pursue personal excellence. A list of tools and resources that she provided me with is listed on the Resources page. She has been instrumental in helping me to strengthen my emotional intelligence and leadership skills. Because of Cindy's coaching, I met the author in me, and I became a much better mother and a confident Christian marketplace leader.

At the time of this writing, it's been almost four years, and I have fully recovered from the stroke. I owe all the glory, honor, and praise to God for how far He brought me. He blessed me with angels to look out for me and helped me regain my memory and learn to live again. As a result of everything I endured, I'm much more compassionate and understanding because many people had to be patient with me while I was in recovery.

Adopt

New mindsets and behavoirs to believe in yourself.

...and Laugh, Smile, Encourage Yourself,

Play, Color, Eat Well, Rest, Give & Forgive!

CHAPTER 27

Your Story. Adopt

If you have suffered from a trauma that has left you feeling aggrieved, victimized, and cast aside, know that there is nothing too hard for God. The same God who healed the woman with the issue of blood and healed me from Bell's palsy and a stroke can also heal you from any physical, mental, emotional, or spiritual trauma.

No matter how low you might feel, just like the woman with the issue of blood, you can reach out and touch the hem of Jesus' garment. He is more than able to heal and redeem you. You will overcome this. You will learn from this. You will use your testimony to help others. Don't let anyone make you feel less-than because of what you're going through. The way I looked and felt because of the stroke bothered me. I didn't even want to leave the house, but I still had to go to work. It's not always easy to keep your head up when faced with blatant criticism by people who don't even know all the details of your situation.

Lean into the people in your life who will motivate you, help boost your spirits, and pray for you instead of talking about you. Know that you can and will make it through this trial and come out on the other side better, stronger, and wiser than you were before. Your recovery will take time. It doesn't happen overnight. Even though I knew I had to work and take care of my children, I also knew that I couldn't effectively do those things without proper rest and rehabilitation. As a working mother, it was challenging to keep my mind and body's need for adequate rest in perspective but doing so was vital to my progress. Intense therapy takes a toll on your mind, so make sure you are getting enough sleep, even napping when you can, because rest is your brain's opportunity to recover and heal itself. Remember that it's not selfish to put yourself first; it's considerate because being healthy will only make you a better woman, mother, wife, friend, daughter, leader, and member of society.

I invite you to look over the next page to help you a**dopt a New Mindset and allow yourself to aspire and make a difference in the world.**

A: **Adopt** a New Mindset

Congratulations, I want you to celebrate the steps you've taken to arrive at this juncture. You know who you are, you've harvested lessons learned, you've released fear, you've enlisted allies, and as you continue to come through your healing, it's time for you to adopt a new mindset.

1. **Ask yourself:**
   - What new habit do I want to start?
   - What old habit do I want to break?
   - How can I think differently?

Use your "Thread Workbook" and begin to jot down answers to the above questions. I've created a worksheet for you with three circles to engage with.

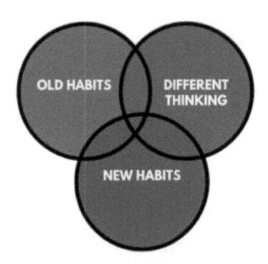

Below are a few additional steps for you to consider reaping even more benefits from your making changes.

2. **Pay attention to your thoughts.** Continue to let go of what you cannot change or control and choose instead to create good intentions. Even when you fail, be sure to honor the purposes of those actions and seek ways to improve and

persevere. The next time you're insecure or tempted to judge yourself or others harshly, stop and reflect, why. Identify which of your fears are expressed in your words, thoughts, and actions. Think about ways in which you can adjust.

3. **Become more self-aware.** You have a right to your health and happiness, and God wants you well. Anything and anyone who stands between you and your total health is not worth your time and energy. Put your progress at the forefront of your mind and cast hindrances aside so they won't stand in your way. Perhaps this a good time to engage in a vision board exercise. A vision board is a powerful visualization tool representing your goals and dreams with pictures and inspirational phrases. It helps you focus on and achieve life goals that make you feel happy by activating the powers of vision and faith God has given you to fashion your dreams into reality. There are free online tools you can use, such as *Personal Vision Board* in your Google Play app store. I've also included a vision board exercise in your Thread Journal.

4. **Improve your insight.** Continue to monitor and eliminate any self-defeating thoughts, ideas, or behaviors that make you feel you can't live an abundant life in Christ because you can. Don't sabotage your recovery; instead, be intentional as your heart and mind daily uplift and encourage you. Use the "Beside Still Waters" devotional to assist you with journaling your patterns while acquiring new skills to help you grow.

5. **Learn new ways to implement lasting changes.** Reading Alejandro Junger's book, *Clean,* aimed at helping individuals reverse disease and sustain lifelong health. Participating in Susan Gregory's 21-day online, Daniel Fast, has changed how I view the food body and my relationship with the one who created me. Don't just alter your diet to lose weight and then go right back to your old habits after you've dropped the pounds. Instead, take small steps to help you to prevent health issues down the road.

6. **Leverage existing tools.** Prayer and fasting are vital tools that you can use to help you fight fatigue, defeat, anxiety, worry, and depression. If you don't make time to spend with God, the Enemy will try to infiltrate your mind with his lies. Fight against mental weakness through praying and speaking the Word over yourself.

7. **Dedicate your body—your temple—to God.** When you put your life in God's hands, you'll see God's hands in everything. Your road to recovery may be rugged and steep like mine but know that the end will be a victory for you. Your faith in Jesus Christ is a great starting point for becoming healthy. If your instincts tell you

that something may be off about your body or your overall health, trust them. Don't chalk it up to anything else, put it off, minimize it, or allow shame to keep you from seeking help. I wasn't feeling well when the stroke I suffered ensued, but instead of getting it checked out, I hid in shame, bringing more turmoil and pain to myself in the process. It's only by the grace of God that I survived, and I advise you to learn from my mistakes. Don't ignore the way you feel because you're afraid to face the results.

If you're ready to adopt new mindsets and behaviors and to activate your faith, then pray this simple prayer with me.

* * *

A Pattern to Quilt – Adopt

What this process taught me is captured in this note to you.

Sometimes we receive healing by encouraging ourselves,

smiling,

laughing,

playing,

coloring,

eating well,

giving,

practicing

self-care,

waiting,

loving people to God,

loving on ourselves,

extending forgiveness,

embracing peace,

activating our faith.

Remain committed to moving forward to receive your healing, and before you know it, you'll be up on your feet again.

A Prayer to Adopt

Father, Thank You so much for how You have shown me that healing and recovery are possible.

Thank You for protecting and preserving my life and for not allowing the trauma to ruin me. Lord, please help me find my hope, joy, and peace in You.

Remind me always that I am filled with Your Holy Spirit, and don't allow my circumstances to take away my strength, happiness, or purpose.

Please help me adopt a new mindset and behaviors that will assist me in my recovery physically, mentally, spiritually, and emotionally.

Help me activate my faith in the healing power of Jesus Christ, knowing that He has the power to make me whole again.

I thank You that there is nothing too hard for You. By believing in Your power and utilizing resources to overcome my traumatic experiences.

I declare I am stronger and wiser every day.

In Jesus' name, Amen.

Time to Adopt & Reflect

....
....
....
....
....
....
....
....
....
....
....
....
....
....
....
....
....
....
....
....
....
....
....
....

....
....
....
....
....
....
....
....
....
....
....
....
....
....
....
....
....
....
....
....
....
....
....

SECTION 6

STEP 6. – DREAM

CHAPTER 28

Dream of a New You

Dream Big and Hold Those Dreams in Your Heart

Have you dreamed so big that it scared you to voice your vision? Have you shared your dream with someone to be told that it was too far-fetched or impossible to achieve? Have you imagined more for your life but didn't feel like it could happen?

A dream is a cherished desire, ambition, or aspiration. As children, we dream with no limitations, but as we experience life, our dreams diminish. But dreams give us something to look forward to and pursue. According to Tommy Barnett in *Charisma* magazine,

> *"Dreams are not merely the nightly thoughts you experience as the brain sorts out the day's events. They are the goals and visions that fire your heart and saturate your soul with joy at the very thought of them. They are those continuing visions of what you want your life to be at its highest level of fulfillment—what you want to do, how you want to do it, what kind of person you want to become in the process.[1]"*

Walking in your God-given purpose requires you to dream big and believe that God is faithful in blessing you to do remarkable things.

> *"Never doubt God's mighty power to work in you and accomplish all this. He will achieve infinitely more than your greatest request, your most unbelievable dream, and exceed your wildest imagination! He will outdo them all, for his miraculous power constantly energizes you."*

> *(Ephesians 3:20, The Passion Translation).*

The idea that God will achieve even more than my most unbelievable dream makes me want to dream bigger. It excites me to know that God wants nothing more than to bless me so I can be a blessing to others. And he wants the same for you. Your purpose is so much bigger than you are, so don't limit what God can do in your life by dreaming small. Dream big. Expand your horizons and watch God enlarge your territory.

Sometimes, we allow ourselves to believe the lie that we aren't worthy of having or becoming more because of our circumstances. Don't be afraid to dream beyond your situation because anything is possible. Now is the time to dream bigger and better than you ever have before, so don't hold back. Don't tell yourself that your dreams can't happen because of what you've done or what happened in your past. It takes courage to dream big and walk boldly toward your dreams. You are worthy of so much more than you've allowed yourself to believe, and God wants to bless you in ways you won't have room enough to receive.

As you dream bigger and believe that God will provide more, let Him fill your heart with the dreams and desires that He wants you to fulfill. Welcome His will for your life and open your mind and your spirit.

"Many are the plans in a person's heart, but it is the Lord's purpose that prevails."

(Proverbs 19:21, New International Version).

Allow God to show you the dreams He wants you to pursue so you won't waste time on things and people that God has not ordained for your life. *Charisma* magazine lists these six ways to know if a dream in your heart is from God:[2]

1. **Your dream is more significant than you**: God never gives you a vision that starts and ends with you. He wants to use you to help others. As you pursue the dreams God has placed inside your heart, you'll realize that even if it started out seeming to be about you, God would show you how those dreams will bless someone else. For example, God may give you the dream of leaving your job and starting your own business. While that business blesses you with financial freedom, it may also bless others who will become your employees or benefit from your enterprise.

2. **You can't let your dream go:** When a dream is God-given, there's no escaping it. You may set it to the side for a while or even forget about it, but somehow God will always bring your dream back to your mind. Your dreams are directly connected to your purpose, so just like the purpose that God has invested in you, the dreams He places in your heart will chase you down. You may even want to quit sometimes because dreams don't always come easy, but something inside you will push you to start over or try again. That's the Spirit of the Lord, pushing you to fight for your dream and not give up.

3. **You would give everything for your dream**: Sometimes, your dreams will require sacrifice. I moved across the country to follow the dream I knew God had placed in my heart, and I'm so glad I was willing to listen to His voice, even when

it went against everything I knew and loved at the time. Remember that anything you sacrifice or exchange for the dream God calls you to is well worth the risk. God will return what you lost or gave up, and then some.

4. **Your dream will last forever:** Because the dreams God gives you are bigger than you and are for the expansion of God's kingdom, the results will last forever. In this lifetime and the next, God will bless you for your obedience and your willingness to let Him use your dreams for His glory. The results may take weeks, months, or even years to manifest, but be encouraged that your faithfulness will be rewarded for eternity.

5. **Your dream meets a need nobody else has met:** Sometimes, you'll tell yourself that the dream you have has already been achieved by someone else or that it's not important, which couldn't be further from the truth. Any dream God gives you, there will be room for. Even if someone else is doing it, they aren't doing it the way God intended for you to do it. Be confident in the dream that God has given you, and let nothing or anyone make you feel as though your dream isn't needed and valued.

6. **Your dream brings glory to God:** This is the most important reason God gives us a vision wrapped up in your dream.

"So, whether you eat or drink, or whatever you do, do all to the glory of God."

(1 Corinthians 10:31).

We were put on this earth for one core purpose: to bring glory to God. God gives us all unique talents, gifts, dreams, and callings that help us glorify and honor Him in diverse ways. By fulfilling your God-given dreams, you'll inspire others to love and serve Jesus Christ. There is no greater purpose we could ever fulfill than to bring glory to His name. What dreams are stirring in your mind and heart? Write them down. For, the Word of God says,

Write the vision; make it plain on tablets, so he may run who reads it.

(Habakkuk 2:2.)

Writing your dreams you envisioned for your future will give you something to look forward to and keep you encouraged, even when you must wait for the results to manifest.

In this chapter, we'll be looking at a woman named Rahab, whose story can be found in the Old Testament, the book of Joshua Chapter Two. Rahab wanted to break free from her lifestyle, but God used that dream and made something so much bigger than she was - Jesus would come from her bloodline. Even though pursuing her dream was dangerous, she:

1. **Stayed focus on the dream** she had and didn't let it go because she was ready for a change.
2. **Sacrificed everything** she knew and loved to go after this dream, and it lives on forever in the Word of God
3. **Strategized a plan** that included going after her God-given dream, and she did something that no one else could do, bringing glory to God.
4. **Stayed the course and** rose from a disgraceful position to become a woman of honor and integrity.

As we move through this chapter, allow God to take every thread of your life, no matter how dark or disgraceful it is, and weave it in such a way that despite what you've done or what has happened to you, you'll still fulfill the dream and purpose that God created just for you.

CHAPTER 29

The Story of Rehab

Always remember you have within you the strength, the patience, and the passion for reaching for the stars to change the world.[3] In Joshua 2, Rahab was a Hebrew woman who lived in Jericho's city when the Israelites traveled to the Promised Land. She was a harlot or prostitute, but God used her to help the Israelites conquer Jericho.

I'm intrigued that God chose Rahab and used the thread of her dishonorable career to assisting the Israelite spies to investigate Jericho's military strength. This chain of events saved the Israelite spies' lives and helped bring Israel into the Promised Land. Rahab made a radical decision, took the risk of pursuing her dream to be free of her shameful lifestyle, and used her degrading thread to take positive action.

After Moses died, God appointed Joshua to lead the Israelites into the Promised Land. However, they couldn't get past Jericho's walled city.

"And Joshua, the son of Nun, sent two men secretly from Shittim as spies, saying, 'Go, view the land, especially Jericho.' And they went and came into the house of a prostitute whose name was Rahab and lodged there."

(Joshua 2:1).

This verse tells us that the two young spies ended up in Rahab's house once they reached the city. However, they weren't visiting her to solicit sex as we would expect of two young men when they came to the city. Jericho's people knew Rahab was a harlot and that men always visited her home. This would make the perfect cover story for being in the city.

Of course, God knew Rahab was a prostitute, but He didn't redirect the spies to keep them from going to her house. Rahab heard how God freed the Israelites from their bondage of slavery in Egypt and knew He had parted the Red Sea to allow the Israelites to cross on dry land. She heard that once they arrived safely on the other shore, the Red Sea had come together and drowned the entire Egyptian army that pursued them. As a result, she believed in the God of the Israelites, and she confessed this to the spies.

"For the Lord your God, he is God in the heavens above and on the earth beneath."

(Joshua 2:11).

Because she confessed her belief in Him, God used her shameful lifestyle, her thread at the time, for His divine purpose. He knew she would allow Him to take the wrong in her life and repurpose it for His glory.

Jericho's king was informed that two young men were there to spy on the city so the Israelites could conquer it and that they were seen entering Rahab's house. The king sent word to Rahab and ordered her to turn the young men over to him. However, she hid the spies on her rooftop and responded to the king in this manner:

"True, the men came to me, but I did not know where they were from. And when the gate was about to be closed at dark, the men went out. I do not know where the men went. Pursue them quickly, for you will overtake them."

(Joshua 2:4–5).

Rahab sacrificed her safety to protect the men because she knew her dream of breaking free of her life as a prostitute was divinely connected to helping them secure their safety. She was no fool. Although her career was a dark thread that resulted in her being shunned socially, her occupation made it easy for men to connect with her. Most of the men who came to her were soldiers or merchants who visited places and nations that the children of Israel encountered. They were knowledgeable about the things that happened throughout Israel and told her about them.

Rahab was an intelligent, well-informed, and strategic thinker who used her insight to her advantage. Lying to the king was dangerous. But she had heard that the God of the Israelites was the one true God and that He would overthrow Jericho and deliver the city into the hands of the Israelites. She quickly devised a plan and asked the spies for a favor in exchange for hiding them. Rahab's request that they saved her family when the spies raided Jericho wasn't selfish. Rahab dreamed of breaking free from being a harlot and all that came with it. She dreamed of an honorable life that gave glory to God.

After Rahab and the spies reached an agreement and devised a plan to save her family, she needed to get them back to the Israelite camp outside of Jericho. Her home was built into the city's outer wall, so she helped them escape by letting them down the side of the city wall with a rope hanging out her window. Before the spies left her, they instructed her how to save herself and her family:

"Behold, when we come into the land, you shall tie this scarlet cord in the window through which you let us down, and you shall gather into your house your father and mother, your brothers, and your entire father's household."

(Joshua 2:18).

Rahab obeyed, and when the Israelites invaded Jericho, the scarlet cord was in her window, so her thread continued.

"So, the young men who had been spies went in and brought out Rahab and her father and mother and brothers and all who belonged to her. And they brought all her relatives and put them outside the camp of Israel. And they burned the city with fire and everything in it. Only the silver and gold, and the vessels of bronze and iron, they put into the treasure of the house of the Lord. But Rahab, the prostitute, and her father's household and all who belonged to HER; Joshua saved alive. And she has lived in Israel to this day because she hid the messengers whom Joshua sent to spy out Jericho."

(Joshua 6:23–25).

Rahab was criticized, but she overcame her disgraceful past. She dreamed bigger and used her experience and faith in God to help others, secure her way out of a scandalous lifestyle, and rescue her family. She helped open the door to the entire nation of Israel's promise, purpose, and vision.

Likewise, when we use our experiences and dreams—our threads—meaningfully and put our faith into action, it allows for transformational change to happen. We experience the change we want to see in our lives and help bring positive change to others' lives.

The full realization of this new purpose is finally told in Matthew 1:5, where Rahab is listed in the genealogy of Jesus. Yes, a former prostitute is in the genealogy of Jesus Christ. Rahab was King David's great-great-grandmother.

But what if Rahab hadn't used the dark thread of her reputation for good? What if she had thrown the young spies out or turned them over to the king because they hadn't come to her home to pay for sex? Well, God's ultimate purpose for Rahab's life wouldn't have been revealed if she hadn't adopted her mindset to have faith in God. Because she allowed God to replace the dark thread of her reputation with the golden thread of her belief, He created a magnificent new pattern for her life.

When we stay connected to our thread, God can use us to link others. Rahab surrendered her unwanted threads to God, and God used her in the best possible way. God chose her and gave her a dream to pursue. The fulfillment of that dream is still a blessing to this day. This is an excellent example of why people need to stop being critical and judgmental of others. We don't see their hearts, and we don't know the person's entire situation, but God does.

"For the Lord sees not as man sees: man looks on the outward appearance, but the Lord looks on the heart."

(1 Samuel 16:7).

Anyone with a negative opinion of Rahab would have seen the two young men go into her house, and they might have said, "Oh my! I can't believe that whore! Two men just went in at the same time!" Because of her label as a harlot, many would consider her the least likely candidate for God to choose, but we don't have to be perfect for God to use us. God sees the heart, and He will use whoever He chooses to use. He is God, and He is sovereign.

CHAPTER 30

My Story. Believing in a Dream

"I will listen to what God the LORD will say, for He will surely speak peace to His people and His saints; He will not let them return to folly."

(Psalm 85:8).

Believing in a Dream that Transcends Time

It's one thing to dream, and it's another to put it into a plan of action and start doing. It's not enough to dream differently. You must trust God to put wings on the revelation He has given you. If you believe God gave you a dream and want to experience its manifestation, you must take the first step to move forward and make it happen.

Like Rahab and many others, I've had labels on me because of some poor decisions I made and the consequences I suffered. These labels left me feeling as though I didn't have the right to dream big. After my divorce, I wasn't sure what life would be like as a single mother, raising three children independently. I wanted nothing to do with God at that point in my life. Going through the divorce made me feel like an outcast. Some married couples I once spent time with shunned me. Many told me they could no longer be in a relationship with me since I was now single. Others would use every opportunity to remind me of who I was and what I did.

But God gave me a dream to relocate with my children to a new place and start over. That was met with a lot of opposition, but I didn't allow any naysayers or the Enemy to stop me from fulfilling my dream, finding my purpose, and living out my destiny with intention. I had carried the shame for so long, but I decided it was time to pursue my purpose. This finally prompted me to say, "Enough is enough!" And rid me of my past baggage because I refused to bring it with me into my new beginning. There were still times when I became distracted, and I learned that any time you focus on God and the purpose He has destined for you, the Enemy will attack you as hard as possible to keep you from moving forward.

I was a people-pleaser who over-identified with others in excessive and inappropriate ways, which was one weakness. I went through a period where I allowed everyone who came into my life to take something of great significance from me spiritually, physically, financially, or emotionally. I accumulated quilt scraps where I saw myself as a people-pleasing, giving harlot who allowed friends and foes to come into my life and take what they wanted. I once wiped out my bank account and handed over thousands of dollars in cash to people who pretended they cared, only to have them squander all that I had. They left me broken and bruised by hurtful actions. I worked double-overtime trying to keep up with paying people to love me and be my friend until I could no longer afford this soul-draining lifestyle.

I struggled with my faith and fell many times. After my divorce, I entered a new relationship, and unfortunately, it became emotionally, financially, and physically abusive. This experience felt familiar and made me realize I was liable to repeat the same story as before. Patterns from my past showed up again in another way. This time, instead of sexual abuse, it was physical abuse, manipulation, and controlling behavior. I didn't want to find out how that story ended, and I cut the cord completely from that toxic relationship that made me think I wasn't worthy of anything better. My relationship journey has led me to write my next book, "Riding the Dating Horse: A Journey of Self-Discovery."

I felt a deep sense of unworthiness, disappointment, and emptiness, and I was again contemplating suicide. The car radio was on, and I heard a minister say, *"Prodigal son, come home."* Hissing through my teeth, I quickly turned the radio off and avoiding the message; I hurried inside the house. While in the living room, I turned on my television and on came a female minister. She, too, repeated this phrase, *"Prodigal son come home, and if you come home, God will turn your life one hundred percent around. Just come."*

I felt unworthy and could not accept or believe that God would want to do anything with me. I felt dirty. I felt messy. I felt like nothing.

I struggled, stumbled, and staggered many times to get back up from the discouragement and defeat of unmet expectations. I turned the television off in my state of pain and disappointment and trashed my house in torment. I broke the TV. I smashed all the glassware I could find. I needed to take out my anguish. Starting to trash the furniture in frustration, I heard a small cry. A still, small voice that felt safe, say, "Just come." I heard God calling me to come home. He told me I no longer fitted into the old story that I was holding onto so tightly. He said I was a masterpiece and that if I allowed Him to, like Rahab, He would show me how to use what I had considered useless and unworthy for His glory and my good.

My turning point came when I stopped and went back into the living room. I fell to my knees and screamed out for help. The neighbors thought something was wrong and called the police. When they arrived, they did not know what to believe. The house was trashed, and I was a mess on the outside. I relinquished a piece of myself to that traumatic experience. I cut off my hair and vowed never to grow it again, as I found myself at rock bottom once more.

Mirroring the story of Ruth, my kinsman-redeemer showed up. I accepted His offer of a brand-new start and could slowly rise above my wounds, shame, and failures to re-purpose the scraps and use them as part of my toolkit for the service of the greater good. I dreamed again and believed God would provide a better life for my children and me.

"In the words of King Solomon, 'For the lovers of God may suffer adversity and stumble seven times, but they will continue to rise over and over again."

(Proverbs 24:16-18, The Passion Translation).

This time I also took some time to lick my wounds, put wings on my faith, and step out of my comfort zone to walk into what God promised me because I was still getting to know the woman I was becoming in God.

At this point, and with no effort, the West Coast company reached out to me about a position and hired me. I struggled with my faith and had to be constantly reassured by God that He wanted my children and me to relocate. I seized my opportunity to leave my past behind because I knew deep down that God led me to pursue this dream of a new life. I felt confident trusting Him and placing my faith in pursuing everything He offered. God will expose us to what greatness looks and feels like if we're brave enough to step out and obey Him even when we do not understand what He is doing.

One day, as I read Rahab's story, I noted how she had a dream even after everything she had done. She became the architect of her life instead of succumbing to her circumstances. I noted the strategy she used to get out of the toxic environment that abused her and negatively labeled her. After reading her story, I came to my senses and made the bold decision to solicit God's help through prayer and fasting. I needed the power of God to take over my life, guide my path, and inspire me to wake up from my dream and start doing what He created me to do. I communicated my needs to God, surrendering all my cares and concerns to Him.

After re-focusing on my connection with God, I embarked on another spiritual journey as part of my Twenty-one-day, Daniel Fast, which I was determined to finish strong. I did! During my time with God, I read the book Experiencing God: Knowing and Doing the Will of God by *Claude V. King* and *Henry Blackaby.*

I engaged in a deep conversation with God and asked Him, "Lord, please confirm to me why you created me?" As plain as day, the Lord told me He called me to write, teach, and speak His word to millions. I laughed to myself as Sarai did in Genesis 18:12 after Abram shared the news that she would be the mother of many nations. I thought:

142

How will this ever come to fruition, knowing my past? I felt unworthy, inexperienced, and unqualified to speak to people, let alone inspire them. I felt unable to fulfill the purpose God had given to me. However, just like Rahab had a God-given revelation that the Israelite God was the true and living God, God gave me my revelation about my future, and I chose to believe Him. I started praying and seeking God, and I went on another fasting- and-prayer, spiritual retreat with God, completing it in fifteen days. No matter your past mistakes, God can transform them into a message of hope, a lantern to lead someone out of the darkness.

God worked everything out for my good and His glory, and He completely transformed my life. He turned the wounded girl into an award-winning business leader. The desperate college drop-out teen mom is now a deliberate and wildly creative university professor. The injured woman is now an inspirational author and speaker. Here are a few ways that He has helped me take the six steps outlined in this book, and in doing so, I sew a better tapestry, and so can you. I;

Adopted a new mindset to motherhood and enjoying the adventures of raising three beautiful women of God.

Obtained an MBA and a Ph.D. degree while healing through neurological disorders.

Released over 100 lbs. of unwanted weight and created healthy behaviors to forge my life forward.

Became a university professor and have taught thousands of graduate and undergraduate students' various courses.

Won the elite "40 under 40" Pacific Coast Business Times award for one of the best transformational leaders on the Central Coast

Authored and self-published books to help women heal from trauma, and one became a #2 Amazon Best Seller!

Partnering with local and national prison ministries to use this self-help toolkit to help women behind bars make better decisions and experience fewer regrets.

Speaking to audiences worldwide and empowering women to rise from trauma and crisis and reclaim their lives.

Leading large-scale organizational and talent development efforts for a government agency with 4,700 employees.

Building a pipeline of the next generation of leaders through cutting-edge training, coaching, and succession planning.

Helping emerging writers manifest their dreams of becoming award-winning authors.

Pioneered a podcast program for an organization that serves over 479K community residents.

Writing trauma-informed care books and developing tools, programs, and resources to help individuals, teams, and organizations achieve intentional transformation.

The power of God can shift things in our favor so we can fulfill our purpose and bring glory to God. Tag, you're it. Rise, go after your dreams and experience what the power of God and you can do.

"Brothers and sisters, I know that I have not yet reached that goal, but there is one thing I always do. Forgetting the past and straining toward what is ahead, I keep trying to reach the goal and get the prize for which God called me through Christ to the life above."

(Philippians 3:13–14, New Century Version).

My vision for the future is to reach millions of hurting women and assure them that God can repair, heal, and restore their lives.

If you want to experience a breakthrough, be willing to take risks and step out on your journey with God.

You can only reach inner peace when you practice forgiveness. Forgiveness is letting go of the past and is, therefore, the means of correcting our misperceptions.[4]

How did I rediscover myself? Stepping away from what I thought I wanted, taking baby steps to allow God to heal me and show me how to use the power of intentionality to choose the desired outcome I want to achieve in every situation... In that process, I discovered how to cut the shackles connected to my past mistakes and make a new commitment to honoring and celebrating my worth. In the words of King Solomon,

"He that getteth wisdom loveth his soul: he that

keepeth understanding shall find good."

(Proverbs 19:8, King James Version).

After hearing *Lisa Nichols* speak during one of her seminars, I started a twenty-one-day practice. I would look myself in the eye, place my hands over my heart, and with no self-judgment, I asked and received God's forgiveness, my commitment, and celebrated. Feel free to replace my name with yours as you declare:

Lord, forgive me for not accepting myself completely.

Thank you, Lord, I am forgiven.

144

THE THREAD

Lord, forgive me for allowing others to corrupt my mind into thinking

I wasn't good enough.

Thank you, Lord, I am forgiven.

Lord, forgive me for lowering my standards and seeking love

and acceptance in all the wrong places.

Thank you, Lord, I am forgiven.

Lord, forgive me for letting people take advantage of me and letting loneliness cause
me to mistake lust, lies, and manipulation for love.

Thank you, Lord, I am forgiven.

Lord, forgive me for ignoring the warning signs and for not

trusting my discernment.

Thank you, Lord, I am forgiven.

I also honored my commitment to the woman I was becoming through positive self-
talk:

Leonie, I commit to valuing myself and that my "yes" will be a

true "yes" and my "no" will be a firm "no."

Leonie, I commit to pressing stop on the negative self-talk.

Leonie, I commit to letting go of living in torment from past failed relationships.

Leonie, I commit to loving you always and will be OK with your crying when you feel
sad.

Leonie, I commit to lightening up and not coming down so hard on you.

I celebrated with love the woman who was taking small steps to write a better next chapter in her life story:

Leonie, I celebrate you for getting out of bed today.

Leonie, I celebrate you for showing up and operating with excellence at work.

Leonie, I celebrate you for seeking help to heal, as I celebrate you for writing and sharing your story with the world.

Leonie, I celebrate your modeling self-care, self-love, and healthy boundaries.

Leonie, I celebrate you for knowing, believing, and appreciating the fact that your very existence is enough!

You can rise above your limitations and self-defeating thoughts to stand in the place of possibilities. There is plenty of room for pioneers of the possible, history makers, navigators of the unknown, change agents, and trailblazers in that space. God remains the same.

He is the creator of life, the author of purpose, and the remodeler of old into new.

Dream

....Of a new you. Dream big.

...and Dream

...with passion and determination. Have faith and believe!

CHAPTER 31

Your Story. Dream

When, we are set free from the bondage of pleasing others, when we are free from currying others' approval, then no one will make us miserable or dissatisfied. And then, if we know we have pleased God, contentment will be our consolation.[5] God's message for you is waiting to be uncovered, and you will need to discover it. You're not a chess piece; you're an essential part of God's kingdom, and you are blessed.

"Was not Rahab the harlot justified by works when she had received the messengers and had sent them out another way? For as the body without the spirit is dead, so faith without works is dead also."

(James 2:25–26, New King James Version).

Rahab had faith, and she used it to pursue her dream, and you can do the same. You have the power to use the dreams God has given you to bless yourself, your household, and others—and move from shame to generational fame. Fulfilling your dreams won't come by chance, and they require deliberate actions. You can only cultivate their results through inspired actions and bold steps, and not by chance. God had a purpose for Rahab's life, but Rahab had to fulfill her role to walk in that purpose. Through obedience, she successfully turned her shame into a shower of blessings, transformed her shambles to shining light, and navigate from poverty to stardom through God's grace. If there is life, there is hope. There is no unusable man or woman on earth. None!

Don't evaluate yourself through others' perspectives, as others' opinions will impede your progress, mission, and derail your dream. Not everyone will understand your purpose and will have different ways of achieving things. Don't let them hinder you because you aren't following the same step-by-step process others have used to reach the same goal. And don't allow others to distract you from your end goal. Instead, be present. Appreciate where God is taking you and enjoy the ride! Know that God has planned and knows every step you will take on your journey to manifest your dream-centered purpose.

Rahab used her experience—her thread—to transform her life. God formed and marked YOU for a specific purpose. He knitted you in your mother's womb and orchestrated that you would read this book at this time in your life. He wants your life remarkably transformed by His amazing grace.

Like Rahab, you may have felt like an outcast in the eyes of a man. But God hasn't changed his mind about you, canceled your destiny, or disqualified your dream because of your mistakes. He is the author and the finisher of our faith. You don't have to try to make things happen with your strength. Take a chance and step out in faith!

If you want God to do something for you, take Him at His word! Use the threads of your life, all that you've been through, and all the tears you've shed and sewed it into your journey. Sew it into your purpose. Rahab took charge of her faith, stepped out, and asked for what she wanted. It's time for you to do the same.

The only person who can pull me down is myself, and I will not let myself pull me down anymore.[6] keep from making the same mistakes and rise above them; it's vital to take an honest look at what is and isn't working in your life. It's time to dream differently and seize your opportunity to walk in purpose.

Ask what you want God to do in your life. How often do you ask for what you desire directly, boldly, and clearly? How often do you ask without shame, guilt, apology, or passive-aggressive hinting? Sometimes your need is obvious. Other times, it's deeply hidden. When we stay silent, or when we ask in hesitation, we victimize ourselves.

"Until now, you've not been bold enough to ask the Father for a single thing in my name, but now you can ask and keep on asking him! And you can be sure that you'll receive what you ask for, and your joy will have no limits."

(John 16:24–26, The Passion Translation).

The first step is to believe that everything is possible with God (Matthew 19:26). Then invite God to intervene and take over in your life. Build a relationship with Him. Talk to Him and read His Word. What do you want from God? Once you know what you want—a miracle, healing, a job, a new car, marriage, children, freedom from addiction—ask for it. Align your wants with God's will and purpose for you. Make it crystal clear what you're asking for, even in situations that seem impossible. You don't have to settle for less than God's best for you. You show up and illuminate your light so others can see their way out of the darkness.

God knows the secret petitions of your heart, but He wants you to bring them to Him. Instead of looking to others for solutions to your personal life experiences, open your mouth and talk to God, who is the manufacturer of your life. God loves you. He speaks, He knows, He answers, He guides, and He provides. Let God show you how to turn scraps into treasure. Let's explore the final step, which is intended to help you to…

* * *

D: DREAM of a New You

T-H-R-E-A-D

Ask yourself:

- What life do I want?

- Who am I six to twelve months from today?

- Who are my friends?

- What are we doing?

- What achievements am I celebrating?

- What is the first step I need to take to bring my vision to life?

- Take action.

Many different issues can keep you stuck in the past and hold you back from dreaming differently and big. Shame, impatience, pride, lust, covetousness, bitterness, anxiety, and mediocrity are all weights. If left unattended, they will distract us, hinder our ability to hear God, weigh down our hearts, deplete our energy, and distance us from our dreams. If we want to grow in our purpose, we must let go and believe in God's will for our path.

"Let go of every wound that has pierced us and the sin we so easily fall into. Then we will be able to run life's marathon race with passion and determination, for the path has been already marked out before us."

(Hebrews 12:1, The Passion Translation).

Congratulations!

You know who you are, you've harvested lessons learned, you've released the things that no longer serve you, you've enlisted allies to support you, and you've adopted a new mindset. Now, the ultimate step is to design and welcome the new you into your hold today.

invite you to use the list of things from Step three of Chapter 17 (see page 81) from our "keep" list. Examine it and add it to the list if needed. Use the items on this list to polish and cherish those things that build the new you— a Daughter of God. Now stand in your awareness. Recognize the knowledge you have garnered from the lessons that your past mistakes have taught you. If you find yourself staring down at the road in front of you, wondering how to find the strength to manifest your vision for the future, know anything is possible. Be your authentic self, keep learning, make a vision board, pray, have faith, and believe in yourself.

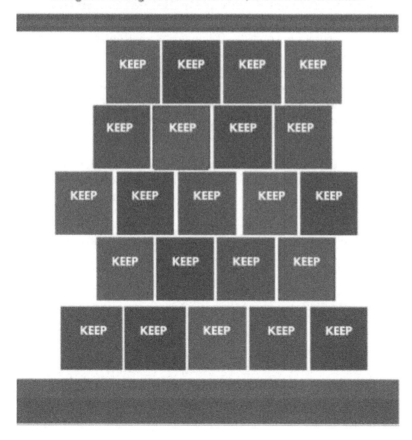

THINGS YOU WANT TO TAKE TO JESUS

Prayfully list the things that will enable you to make positive change for lasting sucess. Remember, it is....transformation

We base many of our present fears on the distorted ways we look at ourselves and our past. Resist every thought that makes you feel you cannot overcome your past and then follow your dreams and walk in purpose. You have the power to overcome and release those thoughts by declaring what the Word of God says about you and striving to please God in everything you do.

Speak life to your situation. Consistently meditate on encouraging thoughts found in the Word. Connect with the love of God and be willing to let Him define you, not your experiences. Practice declaring the promises of God over your life. Know that you were created to fulfill a purpose. Passionately believe everything God says you can have and invest in the dreams He has shown you. Be deliberate and stay consistent about spending meaningful time with God. Be satisfied with all that God is and has done for you through His Son Jesus. Speaking words of affirmation is a beautiful way to teach yourself to think positively, feel confident, and live a happy life. Every day, tell yourself what you need to hear to move your life forward. By doing this, you'll become your source of motivation, positivity, happiness, and hope.

Live your purpose and enjoy the adventure. God is the one who can make the most significant transformation, and embracing Jesus helps to adopt a new mindset, new habits, and new outcomes in your life. If you are ready to make significant and lasting changes in your life, be prepared to step outside your current way of being and embrace new habits. Create the life you want with your purpose, not someone else's. Your life is your signature creation, and you must live true to yourself. Express yourself boldly, create what you love, love what you create, and enjoy the adventure of chasing down your God-given dreams. Expand and live your vision, and your life will become the most significant and most authentic expression of who you are.

Start a gratitude thread journal. Before you go to bed tonight, write down five things you have appreciated about today. Practice speaking out loud and declare the Word of God over your life. Open up your heart and feel love and appreciation for having survived everything you've experienced.

Use some examples below from the list of personal affirmations to help you engage with the Word of God.

Positive Affirmations

1. *I am significant.*

2. *I am worthy of living the life I was created to live.*

3. *I am a gift to the world.*

4. *I only think of lovely things, the things that are good and honest.*

5. *I can do all things through Christ who strengthens me. All of heaven is supporting me in finishing strong.*

6. *My life experiences are not a curse but a huge blessing to my purpose.*

7. *I refuse to waste my time on negative thinking or others' limiting beliefs.*

8. *I have the power to create the life I want to live. I will fully enjoy my time on*

9. *earth.*

10. *I am not afraid; I have faith. My faith fuels my dreams.*

11. *I honor and celebrate my worth daily. I love the woman I am becoming.*

12. *I brighten the world with my light.*

13. *The people I'm called to serve and work with appreciate me.*

14. *I love myself and others.*

15. *I release fear and reject regrets.*

16. *I achieved my goals.*

17. *I enlist allies to support me.*

18. *I adopt a new mindset and behaviors.*

19. *I live an abundant life in Christ Jesus.*

20. *I am determined and driven.*

21. *I have faith in God.*

22. *I use my gifts for the good of humankind.*

23. *I believe in myself.*

24. *I am focused on my mission.*

25. *I am steadfast in my faith.*

26. *I bring glory to God as I live out my destiny.*

27. *I am a winner in God.*

28. *I do not need anybody's permission to exist.*

29. *I pursue my purpose and live it with intentionality.*

30. *I value my gifts and talents.*

31. *I permit myself to impact the world.*

32. *I am open and receptive to all the wealth God offers.*

As we spend time with God, asking questions, looking to Him for direction, and placing our lives in the eye of His needle, our threads will unfold. As we attend to those unfolding threads and use all our experiences, we take both the joyful and the painful threads to help others. As such, we find life's harmony and peace in how even the darkest aspects of our past can bless others.

Dream A Pattern to Quilt

Your faith will not remove, erase, or reduce the pain of the past, but it will enable you to endure it with patience as you continue to thread the needle for sewing. Your life is a mosaic of God's perfect pattern. Be encouraged by the message the apostle Paul transcribed for us:

"With all this going for us, my dear, dear friends, stand your ground. And don't hold back. Throw yourselves into the work of the Master, confident that nothing you do for him is a waste of time or effort."

(1 Corinthians 15:58, The Message).

Be confident, rise, and free yourself of the shackles of your trauma. And as you go forward, use your thread to mend the tatters, shreds, and scraps of trauma and shame once and for all. It's not enough to have the thread; you need to do something with what you've been given. You can mend your life, and you can mend your heart. You can stitch the scraps others have torn from your spirit back together to create a beautiful quilt of comfort, hope, and peace. God has put enough thread in your needle. It doesn't matter if you're fifteen, thirty, fifty, sixty, seventy, or a hundred. It is never too late to start the sewing process.

You have more strength than you realize, and you have what it takes to bring your dream to life. You have your tenacity, and you've been working hard even when you felt like giving up. You have resilience. You have experience. You have determination, drive, and ambition.

Release every negative mindset and behavior that prevents you from dreaming differently and seizing every opportunity God gives you to fulfill your dreams. Activate your faith in God, and stand by Him so that He will stand by you. Your relationship with Him will sustain you through life's journey. You have what it takes if you believe in God and believe in yourself. He gives you the power to overcome your past and transform it into a life-giving dream that will bless multitudes.

My sister, remain focused on your mission.

My sister, stand your ground in the Lord.

My sister, keep steadfast in your faith.

My sister, press into God and seek first His kingdom.

My sister cast away every doubt.

My sister, wait for the fulfillment of your promise.

My sister, live out your destiny.

My sister receive the joy of the Lord.

My sister remain sober in the Lord.

My sister, rest if you are feeling tired.

My sister, do not grow weary with worry.

My sister do not get discouraged.

My sister do not give up.

My sister, do not lose your focus.

My sister, pursue your purpose and live it out with intention.

Don't let your past stop you from dreaming of bigger and better—May your life overflow with blessings. "So above all, constantly chase after the realm of God's kingdom and the righteousness that proceeds from him. Then all these less important things will be given to you abundantly."

(Matthew 6:33, The Passion Translation).

Chapter 32

Dream of a New You Prayer

Father, I am so grateful for how these words are truly awakening a fire inside of me and showing me, I can and will make a better life for myself out of these scraps.
You have shown me are not useless.
I pray You take the scraps of my life and transform them into useable works of art to help others see how awesome and mighty You are.
I'm Your willing vessel.
Lord, thank You for inspiring me to dream differently and to know that You are eager to bless me with more than I could even imagine.
Thank You for Your Word.
Please remove every remaining shred of guilt and shame that tries to keep me from fully embracing my dreams.
Show me the dreams you have placed in my heart and guide me in fulfilling them.
Thank You that my dreams are bigger than I—that they will last forever, meet someone else's need, and bring glory to Your name.
Please help me do everything unto You and not for my selfish gain.
Thank You for instilling in me the desire to expand my horizons as You enlarge my territory.
I declare my freedom to live true happiness in Christ.
I give You all the glory, honor, and praise.
In Jesus' name. Amen.

A Time to Dream & Reflect

....
....
....
....
....
....
....
....
....
....
....
....
....
....
....
....
....
....
....
....

Section 7

GIFTS & VALUES

CHAPTER 33

Discover Your God-Given Gifts

"We have different gifts, according to the grace given to each of us. If your gift is prophesying, then prophesy in accordance with your faith."

(Romans 12:6, New International Version).

Believing Your Worth

You have now explored the six Steps of the T.H.R.E.A.D System, and I encourage you to go back over and revisit the material. Please do not feel you have to do this in any order. Whichever way works for you. You may find that some Steps are difficult to read. I understand, Be kind to yourself, and do not force the process. Our brains protect us from things that we sometimes cannot cope with. You will find the different materials in the book helpful for you to overcome blockages. For example, take some time just to imagine yourself as the person. Closing your eyes and taking some deep breaths will help you connect with your spiritual self.

As you craft your quilt, you radiate your warmth and abilities, reflecting your worth, values, and spiritual gifts. You have touched on the role of 'values' in the Steps and the accompanying 'Workbooks,' and they are the internal compass that will guide you through life. Your values are informed by your religious beliefs, culture, and THREADS, and they give your life meaning and purpose. Many people find it difficult to identify 'true values' in their life and confuse them with other 'standards.' For example, what is the difference between a value, a principle, a behavior, or a virtue?

The easiest way to consider it is that a value is enduring. It doesn't change over time. A value will guide your behavior, and it is internal and personal to you. Values are subjective, emotional and determine the way you live your life. Looking at this definition, it is easy to see why considering values is so important within the context of the T.H.R.E.A.D. System.

The T.H.R.E.A.D System will guide you towards your life goals and give you the support to reach them. Knowing your values, and honoring them, will help you progress in that direction and remain true. This way, you will feel more settled and confident if life knocks you off course.

As part of the System, you have already started building an effective toolkit that will help you ride the waves of life, knowing that you have God's love and support. Take some time to identify your four most important Life 'Values.'

Exercise: Life Values

Take two sheets of paper and fold them into twelve cards each (3 x 4).

On each of the twenty-four cards, write a 'Life Value' (e.g.)

Cut out the cards and ask yourself. "How important is this Life Value to ME for the quilt to remain the beautiful, warm, and comforting blanket I'm designing it to be? Sort into three piles. 'Important,' 'Not so Important,' 'Not at all Important.'

The aim is to reduce the cards to 3 -4 of the most important cards. When you have done this, you will know what YOUR most important values are.

Remember, living by these values under God's direction will help you focus on your true meaning. Staying true to Life Values reduces your inner turmoil, allowing you to share your values and the gifts God has given you.

Understanding Spiritual Gifts

Once you've dreamed differently, and you've stepped out to pursue the dreams God placed in your hearts, you must also learn how to discover your God-given gifts. Gifts will assist in the fulfillment of your purpose. Each one of your gifts is unique, natural, special abilities that God has given to you so you can flourish in your calling. Just like the dreams God inspires, your gifts are not intended to be solely for your use, but a blessing for many. Your values will guide you and will help you share your gifts with the world.

Pinpointing the gifts God has given to you can challenge you as you have spent so long in turmoil, confusion, and within your tangled web. But God has blessed each of us with gifts He intends for us to grow in every day. As you value your gifts, you bring glory to His name, taking a step closer to excelling in your specific callings. In ROMANS 12, 1 CORINTHIANS 12–14, and EPHESIANS 3, the apostle Paul taught about spiritual gifts and the roles of God the Father who empowers us, Jesus the Son who endorses us, and God the Holy Spirit who teaches us to use the gifts we have been given. Paul also taught, in

ROMANS 12:3–8, 1 CORINTHIANS 12:8–10, EPHESIANS 4:1, and CORINTHIANS 7:7, that of twenty-two spiritual gifts, and these are set out below (GiftsTest.com[1])

The God-Given Gifts

Administration: The gift to enable a natural-born leader great at multi-tasking.

Craftsmanship: Empowers the ability to create and build quality projects.

Celibacy (or the gift of singleness): Motivates and encourages select members of the body of Christ to remain single, at will, and without regret and with the ability to maintain control over sexual impulses, serving the Lord without distraction.

Discernment: Promotes the ability to distinguish between right and wrong and make wise decisions accordingly.

Faith: Gives the gift to believe God will do great and mighty things and understand God's divine ability and strength to fulfill His promises.

Giving: Furnishes wealthy living so one can then bless others with their financial prowess.

Evangelism: Delivers the non-condemning ability to draw non-Christians to Christ through love, understanding, and compassion.

Exhortation: Provides others with the love, support, encouragement, strength, and comfort they need to lead successful lives in God.

Healing: Helps God to use a person to heal others physically, mentally, emotionally, or spiritually.

Help: Grants a person to be supportive in ministry and always ready to assist in any act or area that God assigns.

Hospitality: Gifts an individual to create a welcoming and comforting environment where others can feel at ease being themselves.

Intercession: Moves a person to stand boldly in prayer for others, believing that God will hear and answer their prayers.

Leadership: Affords the ability to guide and positively influence others.

Mercy: Provides with a willingness to forgive, take on the burdens of others, and be empathetic toward them.

Miracles: Cause a person to pray and allow God to use them to perform extraordinary and sometimes unexplainable acts of God.

Pastor/Shepherd: Nurtures the gift of leading God's children, with sensitivity and compassion, into a closer understanding of and walk with God.

Prophecy: Allows the hearing and communicating of divine messages from God.

Serving: Humbles a person to put their needs aside in the interest of other

Teaching: Equips with the ability to learn about, study, and share the message of Jesus Christ to inspire others.

Tongues: Affords speaking in a heavenly language that can only be interpreted through the Holy Spirit.

Wisdom: Bequeths the ability to better understand situations instead of taking them at face value.

Word of Knowledge: Supports a person to deliver the truth through the Word of God.

There's no limit to the number of God-given gifts you can have, but it is important to value and discover the gifts God has given you.

"There are different kinds of gifts, but the same Spirit distributes them. There are different kinds of service, but the same Lord. There are different kinds of working, but in all of them and everyone it is the same God at work."

(1 Corinthians 12:4–7, New International Version).

According to 1 CORINTHIANS 12:6–7, every believer has at least one gift, and we have a responsibility to retrieve our gifts, unwrap them, take them out of the box, grow them, and use them to fulfill the purpose God has created for us as we serve others for the greater good. To discover the gifts God has placed in you, start by thinking about what you're good at or enjoy doing. Examine the list of gifts and see what fits your personality and interests. Peter Wagner's book, *Finding Your Spiritual Gifts Questionnaire: The Easy to Use, Self Guided Questionnaire,* is a great place to find more information about where and how you fit.

Pray and reflect about every gift that resonates within you, and through the leading of the Lord, allow Him to guide you toward your purpose. There may be gifts He wants to draw out of you that you didn't know you had! As you allow God to minister to you regarding the gifts, remember these key facts about your God-given gifts. Paul wrote some of the Bible's most powerful passages about gifts, and the following two passages summarize his writing.

"In his grace, God has given us different gifts for doing certain things well. So, if God has given you the ability to prophesy, speak out with as much faith as God has given you. If your gift is serving others, serve them well. If you are a teacher, teach well. If your gift is to encourage others, be encouraging. If it is giving, give generously. If God has given you leadership ability, take the responsibility seriously. And if you have a gift for showing kindness to others, do it gladly."

(Romans 12:6–8, New Living Translation).

"To one person, the Spirit gives the ability to give wise advice; to another, the same Spirit gives a message of special knowledge. The same Spirit gives great faith to another, and someone else, the one Spirit gives the gift of healing. He gives one person the power to perform miracles and another the ability to prophesy. He gives someone else the ability to discern whether a message is from the Spirit of God or from another spirit. Still, another person is given the ability to speak in unknown languages, while another is given the ability to interpret what is being said."

(1 Corinthians 12:8–10, New Living Translation).

When reflecting on your gifts, you must be honest with yourself about what your gifts are. Every gift is of equal value. No gift is more significant or more important than another. Billy Graham explains this below:

God wants you to discover your gift and use it for His glory. No, yours may not be as public as someone else's gift; not everyone (for example) is called to become a preacher or teacher (although some are). But that doesn't mean your gift is any less important in God's eyes—because it isn't. For example, some people have a God-given gift for encouraging others, being kind or merciful, or giving wise advice to those who need it.[2]

If you think back over each of the examples of women in Steps 1 – 6, you will remember, their gifts were all unique to them. Each woman had a gift to share that could benefit others. You need never be envious of another person's gifts, but celebrate them as they walk in their God-given purpose, knowing that the same God who blessed them with specific gifts has also blessed you with gifts that will bring life to others. Every gift is important and necessary in the body of Christ.

The existence of a gift is a call to exercise it. Paul advised us to use our gifts for the glory of God:

"Do not neglect the gift that is in you."

(1 Timothy 4:14, New King James Version).

This chapter explores Deborah's story, an Old Testament judge and prophetess, and Jael, a soldier's savvy wife. Their Jael stories show us that God will choose and use whom He desires; all we need to have is a willing heart and a mind ready to do what God commands.

"A gift opens the way and ushers the giver into the presence of the great."

(Proverbs 18:16, New International Version).

Let God use the gifts He has given you for His glory, and you'll see how His ways genuinely satisfy you.

Start where you are—do anything you can do, and do everything you can do, until you find something you must do! That something is probably your spiritual gift [3]

CHAPTER 34

The Story of Deborah and Jael

"For God, who said, 'Let brilliant light shine out of darkness,' is the one who has cascaded his light into us—the brilliant dawning light of the glorious knowledge of God as we gaze into the face of Jesus Christ."

(2 Corinthians 4:6, The Passion Translation).

J abin, the king of Canaan, for twenty years had cruelly oppressed the children of Israel, and this how Judges 4 begins. Deborah, a prophet and the judge of Israel during this time, had a great responsibility requiring commitment and humility.

"Now Deborah, a prophetess, the wife of Lappidoth, was judging Israel at that time. She used to sit under the palm of Deborah between Ramah and Bethel in the hill country of Ephraim, and the people of Israel came up to her for judgment."

(Judges 4:4–5).

Bestowed upon her by God, Deborah used her God-given gifts to help people escape calamity. She was granted multiple gifts by God, including administration, discernment, exhortation, leadership, prophecy, and wisdom. She didn't have an inflated sense of self-worth because of her gifts but remained humble to God and allowed Him to work through her, exercising her gifts for His glory.

When the people of Israel cried out to God for help, God used Deborah to deliver a word to Barak, a general in the Hebrew army who was her subordinate. She prophesied to Barak that he must take ten thousand men from the tribes of Naphtali and Zebulun and gather them at Mount Tabor. Then God would draw out Sisera, the captain of Jabin's army, and give the Israelites victory over him and his troops. Barak requested Deborah come with him, and she did, using her gifts of leadership and discernment to glorify God:

"I will surely go with you.

Nevertheless, the road on which you are going will not lead to your glory, for the Lord will sell Sisera into the hand of a woman."

(Judges, 4:9).

Because Deborah allowed God to use her abilities, she provided the opportunity for another woman, Jael, to become a key player in God's grand master plan, using two women to give the Israelites victory over their enemy.

Deborah told Barak the moment to attack, again using her spiritual gifts:

"'Now is the time for action! The Lord leads on!

He has already delivered Sisera into your hand!'

So, Barak led his ten thousand men down the slopes of Mount Tabor into battle."

(Judges 4:14, The Living Bible).

Sisera panicked, leaped from his chariot, and escaped on foot to the tent of Jael. Jael's husband, Heber, lived in peace with Jabin, the Canaanite king, and was Sisera's ally and an enemy of Israel. However, Jael did not share her husband's allegiance to Jabin and Sisera, as she was loyal to Israel.

Jael invited Sisera into her tent, promised him safety and protection, and covered him with a blanket after entering. She made Sisera feel welcome, so he relaxed in the presence of his trusted ally's wife. Little did he know her actions were all part of a strategy that Jael had received from God to help Israel escape the hands of Jabin. Sisera asked Jael for water, and she gave him milk, which brought further comfort to the weary soldier. He told Jael to stand at the tent entrance and instructed her to inform anyone who looked for him he wasn't there. After Sisera fell asleep, Jael drove a sharp tent peg through his temple with a hammer.

"When Barak came by looking for Sisera, Jael went out to meet him and said, 'Come, and I will show you the man you are looking for.' He followed her into the tent and found Sisera lying there dead, with the tent peg through his temples.

So that day, the Lord used Israel to subdue King Jabin of Canaan."

(Judges 4:22–23, The Living Bible).

It's amazing that even though Jael wasn't a soldier, she was the reason Israel was successful over Sisera and Jabin. She was willing to let God use her. Jael also possessed multiple gifts, including discernment, hospitality, serving, and wisdom. Her ability to make Sisera feel at ease in her presence allowed her to prevail over him. She discerned when the time was right and didn't hesitate to conquer him. She knew it was God's will that the Israelites made it safely out of the hands of Sisera and Jabin.

Jael is a beautiful example of a woman who exercised her gifts, doing what she believed was right according to her knowledge and discernment. Her choice was clearly in opposition to her husband's stance. But despite her husband's treaty with the Canaanite king, Jael acted according to her convictions. And not only did Jael make a choice that opposed her husband, but she imposed that choice, altering the course of history for both the Canaanites and the Israelites.[4]

God is all-knowing. He strategically used Deborah and Jael to deliver the Israelites out of the hands of the Canaanites. Both Deborah and Jael discovered their God-given gifts and used them to bring God glory, fulfill His plan, and help others. Before they could do that, they had to identify their gifts and be willing to use them. Their story is a powerful lesson we can learn from to determine our gifts.

CHAPTER 35

Gifting My Story

"For the gifts and the calling of God are irrevocable."

(Romans, 11:29).

Succeeding with Purpose

When I was recovering from the life-changing effects of a stroke, I asked myself where do I go from here? Can I use my life experiences to help myself and others. If so, how will I discover my God-given gifts to heal others and bring glory to God?

Going on intentional fasting, aka God adventures, had become a regular practice for me. During one of these adventures and after reading Rick Warren's book *"The Purpose Driven Life,"* I engaged in an intimate conversation with God. I asked Him the following five questions to gain an awareness of my purpose:

1. Who am I?
2. Why am I here?
3. Who am I called to serve?
4. What do they want and need?
5. How will others change because of my purpose?

The Holy Spirit spoke to me, "You are called to teach, and I call you to speak." I laughed, thinking if I can't even speak properly, how can I talk to people? I questioned whether I truly heard from God? I felt overwhelmed and felt that the assignment was a lot to say yes to. However, I jotted what I heard in my spirit down and also drew a person and the cross, and remembered God saying,

"Your job is to connect people to God."

I asked God, "Prove what you say!"

Then I thought, well, a lot has been poured onto me and to whom much is given, much is also required." Luke 12:48

I landed my two teaching positions, and those positions helped me build my communication skills, emotional intelligence, and public-speaking abilities.

I recognized the gifts God granted me, including administration, leadership, and teaching. This process required bravery and courage because even though I was going through healing, I had to take a risk and step out on faith to teach.

Another of my gifts is exhortation or the gift of encouragement. I love to encourage people. I've also found that when my emotions are down in the dumps, encouraging others shifts my energy and brings me back up spiritually and emotionally. I recorded a voice note on my phone and sent it to one of my mentees, and she was so happy. She exclaimed,

"I felt so encouraged, hearing your voice!" She had no idea I was recovering from a stroke. The lesson I learned. No matter what your present condition, let God use you just as you are. From there, I continued recording podcasts, and I started uploading them online. This gave me more opportunities to speak to others while using my gifts.

As I endeavored to recognize my gifts, I wanted to understand my purpose, so I asked myself:

What excites me?

What am I willing to do, with no one paying me?

The answer was mentorship and encouraging others

I do these things with zeal, not looking for payment in return. I'm now using all my resources to mentor girls and women, and God has blessed me with the necessary tools to fulfill my purpose. He has also given me the gifts of discernment, word of knowledge, and wisdom. Through my relationship with the Lord and practicing discernment, I've become able to decipher whom to let in my life, so I'm not taken advantage of. I do my best to consult the Holy Spirit for direction, confirmation, and peace in every situation and decision.

Do you know what the answer would be if you asked yourself, Who am I? I encourage you to look at Marcus Buckingham's book StandOut that provides you with positive language to describe yourself, helping you understand yourself. You can also check out www. ValuesCentre.com, which might help you answer these questions:

1. Who am I?

2. What are my values?

3. What do I love to do that excites and brings me joy?

4. Whom am I called to serve?

5. What do the people I'm called to serve want and need?

Here is an example of my response to the above.

"I am a devout Christian, author, and organization and talent development practitioner. I value Spirituality, courage, happiness, and meaningful work. As a *Maximizer*, I transform people and organizations to impact the world through research, education, and spiritual care. I'm called to serve trauma survivors and supporters who want and are ready to restore their faith, love, and life. They want to find true freedom, happiness, and closeness with God. Some want to build a relationship with Jesus, but they're hesitant. They may see Jesus as a man, and because they've been through trauma—a rape or some form of abuse by a male figure—they may be reluctant to trust God. By sharing my story and by coming from a nonjudgmental perspective. I help survivors rediscover Jesus and provide or point them to resources to support them to heal strong from trauma—just like I did."

Now here's the sticky question to ask yourself: **How will others change because of my purpose?**

Here's an example that has changed my life forever. I remember a friend and sister in the Lord who had been living in America for many years. She left her daughter behind in her country and couldn't get her here because of immigration restrictions. Her situation was heavy on my heart because she talked about her daughter all the time and desperately wanted to bring her to America. I clearly heard the Lord tell me to help, and initially, I tried to ignore this revelation because I didn't believe I could fulfill this particular instruction. But I obeyed. I reached. I asked for help, and the Lord gave me step-by-step directions on how to reach out to immigration. After seeing the process, my friend's 15-year-old daughter was successfully reunited with her mom, dad, and sisters. The Lord used the gifts He gave me to help make this happen, and everything was done with ease.

When we build a relationship with the Lord, He calls us for an assignment and perfects certain gifts in us. God has gifts made available to us if we show Him we're willing to be obedient when He calls us to act. Don't be afraid to ask God to reveal your gifts and help you successfully use them for His glory.

"Ask, and it will be given to you; seek and you will find; knock, and the door will be opened to you. For everyone who asks receives; the one who seeks finds; and to the one who knocks, the door will be opened."

(Matthew 7:7–8, New International Version).

When God started showing me my gifts, I didn't wait for people to give me a chance to put them into practice. I forged ahead with purpose and stepped out in faith. I started building things for the kingdom of God. I now have a podcast online, a meetup group, and a Bible study group. I don't feel the need to wait because I won't give anyone the authority to approve whom God has called me to be. I stepped out on faith and said, *"Yes, God, I believe that I'm called to do this."* Although I struggled with my faith and doubted God's will for my life many times, I was willing to try, to take slow steps, and use what God gave me to manifest His plan for my life. I valued the gift that God has given to me, and I wanted to gift those values to others.

Before my illness, I had a passion for public speaking. When God placed it on my heart that it was time for me to step into my calling and exercise my gifts,

- I volunteered as a Sunday school teacher, taught basic grammar to adults in my church, helped my siblings complete their degrees, taught at a community college, facilitated training courses at work, and volunteered in the community.
- I sought ways to help others to embrace their gifts and talents and unlock their potential.
- I invested in my development through coaching and contained self-help tools I used to improve my skills.
- I studied and learned from individuals successful in public speaking.
- I was invited to and have spoken at Women Empowering workshops, retreats, and conferences on "Rising from Trauma and Crisis and Reclaim Your Life."

You have the freedom to stand in the truth that you were created for a purpose by God. You were given gifts not to remain dormant but to transform lives. Your gifts matter to the people you're called to serve.

Spiritual gifts are something every believer is given when they receive the gift of salvation. Just as the gift of salvation is by grace through faith, so are the spiritual gifts. Our God is so generous. He is constantly giving us things [5]

You have your gift, and now it is time to commit to using your gift for yourself and others. Whatever you ask of God, first believe He is more than able to do it. If it's according to His will for you to have a specific gift, you have a right to believe it's already yours. It's good to ask others to pray for you, but it's more powerful when you pray for yourself and even take it a step further and write down what you're asking God to do. When God gives you the answer, put it into practice. Use the gifts He has given you to glorify and honor Him. As you see Him moving in your life, share it with others. You can use your gifts in the church, the community, home, work, and wherever else you go.

Discover

God's plan for your life.

...and Discover

...your strength, your purpose, and how you are a gift to the world! Enjoy it! Live it!

CHAPTER 36

Your Story: Gift

For I know the plans I have for you, says the Lord. They are plans for good and not for evil, to give you a future and a hope."

(Jeremiah 29:11, The Living Bible).

A Gift to The World

Now that you've seen the power of discovering your God-given gifts and using them to help others through the examples I have shown you. It's time for you to do the same. Your gifts are going to bless so many lives if you'll only discover what they are and surrender to God's plan for how to pursue and prosper in them. You have something special to offer this world, and God is counting on you to believe in yourself and have confidence in the abilities He's given you. The best part about discovering your spiritual gifts is that you don't have to figure them out yourself. Start by praying, waiting, and trusting God to reveal them to you. Open your mouth and bravely ask God to reveal what He has placed inside of you and how to use it. And remember to listen to the answer.

Marcus Aurelius put it like this: "**Get busy** with **life's purpose**, toss aside empty hopes, **get** active in **your** rescue—if you care for yourself at all—and do it while you can

God knows the spiritual gifts that He has placed in your heart, and He will reveal them to you if you ask Him.

"Call to Me, and I will answer you, and show you great and

mighty things which you do not know."

(Jeremiah 33:3, New King James Version).

This verse tells me that God is waiting to show you the incredible things that He wants to do in your life. However, you must hear His voice and to heed His guidance. Remember that your spiritual gifts are for His glory and purpose, so operating in your gifts appropriately requires your trust and assurance in God. Otherwise, you'll just be spinning your wheels. When you trust God to help you hone and sharpen your gifts, you will be more influential than ever before and will find unspeakable joy in honoring Him. Daughter, your past is behind you.

"Therefore, IF ANY man be in Christ, he is a new creature: old

things are passed away; behold, all things are become new"

(2 Corinthians 5:17, King James Version).

Dream Big, Dream Differently.

It's time to shake off any residue from your past that's still trying to debilitate you. Prepare your heart, mind, spirit, and soul for what God is getting ready to do. In the previous chapter, we discussed dreaming big and dreaming differently, and the same is true for the gifts God has given you. See yourself walking in newness, confidently obeying God's instructions, and no longer worrying about what anyone else has to say about it.

Value and Embrace Your Gifts

See yourself valuing and embracing your gifts and using them to help others. Think and speak positively about what God is getting ready to do in your life as you trust Him to draw out what He's placed in your heart.

Invest in Your Gift

When God reveals your gifts to you, it's not just for you to sit on them and expect Him to do all the work. Absolutely not! God gave them to you for you to work on them. Just like a gardener must get down on their hands and knees and till the soil, working the land day in and day out to reap a plentiful harvest, so you must get down and begin working your gifts. God will help you and be with you every step of the way, but He entrusted you with your gifts for you to invest in them.

Work Every Gift

If you have the gift of craftsmanship, you can get on *YouTube* and begin researching how to improve your skills. If you have the gift of exhortation, start delving into the Word of God; that way, you'll know what it says to encourage anyone God puts into your path successfully. Do you have the gift of leadership? Look for divine opportunities to help manage projects that will nurture individual growth and success for others. If you have the gift of teaching, seek avenues where your clarity and understanding can benefit others to see things more clearly. The goal is to work every gift, which shows God that you appreciate what He has invested in you and that you're willing to do whatever it takes to excel at it.

A Parable of Work

In the parable of the talents found in Matthew 25:14–30, a man traveled to a far country. He gave his three servants money to invest for him while he was gone, according to their abilities, in the modern equivalents of five, two, and one thousand dollars, respectively. The first two servants doubled their investments, and upon his return, the master was well pleased and gave them many more responsibilities for being faithful with the small amount he left in their care. However, the servant who had been entrusted with the one thousand dollars hid the money in the ground for safekeeping, afraid his master would rob him of what he earned. The disappointed master gave the wicked man's money to the servant whom he gave the five thousand dollars, with a message:

"For the man who uses well what he is given shall be given more, and he shall have an abundance. But from the man who is unfaithful, even what little responsibility he has shall be taken from him."

(Matthew 25:29, The Living Bible).

The moral of the story is that it does no good to be selfish, lazy, nonchalant, or prideful with what God has given you because when you give it back to Him, He will bless you tremendously. If you can only identify one gift right now, don't be discouraged. As you work that one gift, using it for the glory of God, He will see your effort and be faithful to bless you with many more responsibilities. Do not despise small beginnings, but let God multiply your efforts.

Avoid comparison and competition. We know that useless competition and comparison is the thief of joy, so don't rob yourself of inner peace and happiness by peeping in someone else's window. God gives everyone gifts that complement their personality and the divine purpose He has for their lives. We all have a purpose God wants us to fulfill, so comparing your unique journey to someone else's will only distract you from the mission God has you for and hinder your progress. In the words of Sarah Jakes Roberts, *"God can't bless who you pretend to be or who you compare yourself to. He can only bless you and the lane that was created for you."*[6] If you stop comparing yourself and focus solely on who God wants you to be, you'll find contentment and fulfillment as you have never known before.

Document your progress. Writing your progress can be a powerful tool in your success story. Write the words God speaks concerning your gift and purpose. Write your goals and what you envision and believe God will do in your life. Write positive thoughts about yourself and what God has placed in your heart. Also, write everything you learn about your gift. Never stop researching, learning, and growing in your God-given gifts, because one of the best things about God is that there is always more. It doesn't matter how many years old (or young) you are; there's still more God wants to do through you. You can even take pictures, make voice memos, or record videos to document your progress. When you look back in a year, five years, ten years, or more, you'll see how much you have grown in your gifts and rejoice at how investing in your gifts and your purpose has touched so many lives.

No matter what you've been through, trust that God has a purpose for carrying you through the pain. The fact that you survived your trauma means you can discover how to re-purpose it and make it work for the greater good. Use the gifts God has given you to articulate, appreciate, and bless others with your breakthrough and testimony. There is no amount of pain you have endured that God cannot use, transform, and rearrange to equip others with the necessary tools to overcome their struggles.

If you're ready to discover your God-given talents and use them to help others, pray this simple prayer with me.

CHAPTER 37

Gifting a Prayer

Father, thank You so much for how You have awakened a fire inside of me that makes me want to thrive in my purpose.

Please show me any hidden, undiscovered, or ignored gifts that You have placed inside of me so I can draw them out and begin working them.

Help me not to compare myself to others or feel that any of my gifts are small or insignificant. I know that every gift and every person has a purpose, so please help me keep my eyes on You and stay in my lane. Thank You for the gifts You have entrusted to me.

Please help me use them to glorify You, and not for any selfish or ulterior motive. Give me the grace to work multiple gifts without becoming burned out or overwhelmed. Thank You for Your hand on my life and for choosing me for Your unique and magnificent purpose. Thank You. I am fearfully and wonderfully made. Thank You I am a child of the Most High God. Thank You for the great and mighty things that are getting ready to come.

In Jesus' name, Amen.

CHAPTER 38

A Pattern to Quilt – Values & Gifts

Y ou, my friend, are on the cusp of greatness. Get excited about what God has birthed in you and how His plan is unfolding, even now. So,

Dear woman,

On the Cusp of Greatness

Forget everything that has been said About your lack of strength

And the weakness accrued

To the tears, you cry.

For you are strong.

Within the center of your soul is the forge That houses every human child.

Look how strong you are!

Such pain you bear for overwhelming joy.

Let the world throw its darts In the face of your strength,

While fear quakes at your foundation.

Life may also cut deep, Leaving scars on your beautiful skin.

Hold on and remain unshaken, As pain precedes unlimited joy.

Keep your heart safe,

Let your tears flow,

But keep your faith strong.

It's just a matter of time.

As every experience breeds, wisdom And every fall is followed by a rising,

Even the night is followed by the day.

All are working together for you.

To become the better version of you:

Refined, renewed, restored,

Let not your heart be darkened, And your beauty swallowed in bitterness.

Ensure that no matter what, The beauty remains in your eyes!

A Time to Reflect on Your Gifts

....

....

....

....

....

....

....

....

....

....

....

....

....

....

....

....

....

....

....

....

....

....

....
....
....
....
....
....
....
....
....
....
....
....
....
....
....
....
....
....
....
....
....
....
....
....
....
....

Dream

...Of a new you. Dream big.

...and Dream

...with passion and determination. Have faith and believe!

Section 8

DESIGN & GROW

CHAPTER 39

Have a Growth Mindset

"In everything we have won more than a victory because of

Christ, who loves us."

(Romans 8:37, Contemporary English Version).

Time, and time again, survivors have demonstrated remarkable resilience. The Paralympics show impressive feats of strength, determination, and grit. And success is not just measured in terms of speed, weights lifted, or miles run. It is in the individual's ability to conquer their trauma, injury, and pain. Also, it is the ability to gain victory over the obstacles placed in their way by circumstance and others. Did you know that you're more likely to respond positively to trauma than you are to be ruined by it? In the 1980s, two psychologists, Richard Tedeschi and Lawrence Calhoun, discovered trauma had the power to change people in fundamental and positive ways. An important finding, and one not shared often enough. The psychologist's contacted over six hundred people, and most survivors reported having greater inner strength than before. They had grown closer to their friends and family members, their lives had more meaning, or they were reworking their lives toward realizing more fulfilling goals.[1]

In Psychology Today, Steve Taylor discusses post-traumatic growth. When talking about those who have lived through life-altering events, such as losing a loved one or a serious illness, he says:

187

They gained a new inner strength and discovered skills and abilities they never knew they possessed. They became more confident and appreciative of life, particularly of the 'small things' that they used to take for granted. They became more compassionate for the sufferings of others, and more comfortable with intimacy, so that they had deeper and more satisfying relationships. One of the most common changes was that they developed a more philosophical or spiritual attitude to life. [2]

Having experienced trauma firsthand, I can attest that it can make you a better person, depending on the person you are. Many of the experiences I've shared with you in this book have been painful and life-shattering, yet my life is much better today than when I was going through the trauma. That's why I'm eager to share my story.

Yes, at one point, I lost my identity to Bell's palsy. Yes, I temporarily lost my speech and the movement of my arms to a stroke. I almost lost my soul to manipulative, toxic, and spirit-crushing relationships. Yet, I'm thankful that each of these experiences exposed me to a more profound knowledge of God, my inner power, along with resilience and the willpower to take control and change my life. I learned to establish safe boundaries and positively impact others.

Real growth begins with your determination to heal from trauma. It's not a free pass to avoid suffering. However, as researchers now know, people can do far more than just heal. Given the right environment and mindset, they can change, using the trauma and suffering as opportunities to reflect, search for meaning in their lives, and ultimately become better versions of themselves. [3]

As you do this, you will find the strength, courage, and desire to share your story with others in similar situations so they, too, can overcome their suffering.

Usually, finding the ability to grow despite trauma will require you to change your mindset. In Carol Dweck's book *Mindset: How You Can Fulfill Your Potential*, she discusses the differences between a fixed mindset and a growth mindset. Compiling decades of research, she asserts that it's not only our talent and abilities that determine our success but our mindset. It is our mindset that we can adjust to fulfill our potential.

People with fixed mindsets dislike challenges and have a fear of failure. They tend to give up easily, shy away from difficulty, and get defensive in the face of constructive criticism. Ultimately, they achieve far less than they would be capable of if they will try. If you have a fixed mindset, difficulties can make you complacent and reluctant to step out and try again. With a fixed mindset, you are much less likely to share your story out of fear of what others will think about you.

People with growth mindsets, on the other hand, are not afraid to try. They look at failure as an opportunity for learning and growth. These individuals embrace challenges, persist in the face of opposition, and use constructive criticism to improve their behavior. They see others' successes as inspiring, not threatening, and fulfill their ultimate potential by continually changing, growing, and progressing.[4]

If you have a growth mindset, you'll see your past difficulties as lessons, not losses. You won't allow any obstacle in your past or your path to keep you from fulfilling your purpose. From this moment forward, do not let your past mistakes, failures, and sufferings taunt you anymore. The Word of God is on your side and is your shield.

You're not who you used to be, and you don't have to be defined by what happened to you. You're a new creation, and God is about to do a new thing in your life.

"Remember not the former things, nor consider the things of old. Behold, I am doing a new thing; now it springs forth, do you not perceive it? I will make a way in the wilderness and rivers in the desert."

(Isaiah 43:18–19).

God is already working in your life in incredible and abundant ways. Trust Him to finish this work and allow Him to use you to fulfill His purpose for your life.

In this chapter, we'll discuss the new testament stories of Elizabeth and Mary, who were both used mightily by God. Mary had to identify her thread, her destiny, which was obedience. Even though she didn't understand why she was chosen to bring our Savior into the world, she willingly obeyed. Many times, we cut short our calling to take on other people's destinies. Yet God wants you to create with the thread you've been given in His will.

CHAPTER 40

The Story of Elizabeth and Mary

Faith in God is the key to trusting Him in every circumstance. Walking by faith means when there are unanswered questions, we can be okay with that because God is in control, and we're determined to trust Him no matter what. Joyce Meyer[5]

Luke 1 introduces a priest, Zechariah, whose wife, Elizabeth, was barren. The couple longed for a child for many years, but they had accepted that they would likely never have one in their old age. One day while Zechariah was in the temple in the Holy of Holies, an angel of the Lord, Gabriel, appeared and frightened him. The angel stepped forth and reassured Zechariah:

"But the angel said to him: 'Do not be afraid, Zechariah; your prayer has been heard. Your wife Elizabeth will bear you a son, and you are to call him John. He will be a joy and delight to you, and many will rejoice because of his birth, for he will be great in the sight of the Lord. He is never to take wine or other fermented drink, and he will be filled with the Holy Spirit even before he is born'"

(Luke 1:13–15, New International Version).

If you were Elizabeth and heard such good news about the son you were to carry, can you imagine how much joy you would have? However, Elizabeth never had the chance to hear this information about her unborn child because Zechariah doubted the message. They were old, and the way God worked in the days of Abraham was no longer common. Corrupt Romans controlled the land of Israel, so people had few encounters with God's faithfulness. Understandably, Zechariah wouldn't have expected something as wonderful as the news he heard.

His disbelief had consequences. Gabriel told him that he wouldn't speak until his wife had given birth. How difficult! Imagine Elizabeth rushing to tell her husband she now carried a baby, but all he could do was make gestures.

When Elizabeth discovered she was with child, she rejoiced but stayed in seclusion for five months. Perhaps it was her way of expressing gratitude to God or maintaining privacy to avoid other women's questions in her community. Also, Zechariah couldn't speak to her, and she now had to learn how to understand everything he attempted to articulate to her. Even though Elizabeth had longed for a baby, I can only imagine how painful it was not to talk about the pregnancy with her husband, who couldn't speak.

"After this, his wife Elizabeth became pregnant and for five months remained in seclusion. 'The Lord has done this for me,' she said. 'In these days, he has shown his favor and taken away my disgrace among the people'"

(Luke 1:24–25, New International Version).

From that point on, things changed. The angel Gabriel visited Mary, who was engaged to Joseph, with his message:

"'Greetings, O favored one, the Lord is with you!' But she was greatly troubled at the saying and tried to discern what sort of greeting this might be"

(Luke 1:28–29).

Gabriel told Mary not to be afraid and that she would conceive and give birth to a son named Jesus, who would then be called the Son of the Most High. Mary asked how this would be since she was a virgin, and Gabriel told her the Holy Spirit would come upon and overshadow her, and the child would be called the Son of God. Gabriel also told Mary that her relative Elizabeth was six months pregnant despite being barren in her old age. Elizabeth would later give birth to John the Baptist.

Mary accepted God's will and determined to serve Him:

"Behold, I am the servant of the Lord; let it be to me according to your word."

(Luke 1:38).

Even though Mary couldn't have possibly understood the ramifications of what God had entrusted her with, she adopted the attitude that she could do it since God believed in her. She humbled herself under His mighty hand and allowed Him to be glorified even though she didn't understand.

Would you be willing to do the same? Could you be obedient even if you don't understand everything God is doing in your life or why He is causing you to take certain steps? Trust and believe that any and every step God is causing you to take will not be wasted. God's plan and timing are perfect, and He will fulfill His divine purpose for your life. It isn't always easy to trust a God you cannot see and a plan that isn't tangible, but Mary's story is proof that trusting Him even in the unknown is always worth the risk.

Mary came to her divine realization by talking with the angel, but Elizabeth didn't have that experience. Gabriel informed Mary that Elizabeth was also with child, and Mary visited her. When Elizabeth heard Mary's greeting, the baby leaped in her womb, and Elizabeth was filled with the Holy Spirit and cried out,

"Blessed are you among women, and blessed is the child you will bear! But why am I so favored that the mother of my Lord should come to me? As soon as the sound of your greeting reached my ears, the baby in my womb leaped for joy. Blessed is she who has believed that the Lord would fulfill his promises to her!"

(Luke 1:41–45, New International Version).

Even though Mary didn't understand her divine appointment's details, she trusted God and used her thread of obedience to support Elizabeth, who needed someone to lean on. Sometimes we find it hard to trust God when we don't know what will happen and how and when it will come to pass. I can only imagine the strength and courage it took for Mary to trust God, even though people looked at her as though she and Joseph had committed adultery and as though she had gotten pregnant out of wedlock. Mary was greatly honored by God but also scorned by many.

This is true of many of us today.

CHAPTER 41

Designing My Story

A Growth Mindset

It took a tremendous amount of courage to share my story, but I was brave enough to do it because I wanted to help others overcome what they were going through. I wanted them to heal and live a life of freedom from past trauma. I believe many people are ready for transformation but feel stuck. It's as though they're standing at the runway of life, and they need a gentle push to move forward and to soar. The ability to give a gentle push is one gift God placed in me. Because of this, I know how to empower people. I can encourage them from the Word of God and my own life experience without judgment.

It's been several years since I allowed God to heal my traumatized heart, help me rediscover my purpose, and stand in my truth as I move toward becoming the woman God created me to be. It has been an incredible journey. Just when I thought my spirit was crushed, when I thought trauma had defeated me, I bounced back.

Trauma has shown me how brave, courageous, resilient, and determined I am. It has been an amazing victory and one that I could only have discovered because of my experiences. Looking back, I'm not sure I could have changed anything, even though there are some things I would love to go back and change. However, I have learned to be thankful for all things through Him.

God did not allow abuses to deplete or defeat me. Instead, He has taught me how to rediscover who I am in Him. I've been able to build a close and loving relationship with God, and I can share my triumphant story of transformation with the world.

Yes, traumatic events and injuries rattle our lives down to the very core of who we are. Even so, God will not leave your heart, mind, or soul in shambles because His word is true:

"After you have suffered a little while, our God, who is full of kindness through Christ, will give you his eternal glory. He personally will come and pick you up and set you firmly in place and make you stronger than ever."

(1 Peter 5:10, The Living Bible).

CHAPTER 42

Design Your Story.

Embrace Your Joyful Freedom

You've probably faced inner struggles like those that Elizabeth and Mary experienced in your life. People may have looked down on you without knowing all the details of your circumstances, but God knows the truth. Are you willing to obey Him as Mary did? Are you ready to enjoy the adventure as Elizabeth learned to do? Are you prepared to find the threads that connect every one of your life experiences that brought you to this moment? To where God is conjoining all the crooked, tainted, dark, messy, unrecognizable threads and crafting His beautiful masterpiece?

He's about to show Himself strong and prove that all along, He knew exactly what He was doing. He is a master craftsman, the very Creator Himself, and He will take everything. The good, bad, and in-between. And he will work it together for the good of those who love and trust in Him.

Do you realize that all of heaven supports us to heal, rise from our pain, take control of our lives, and live out our destiny with intention? Just as with Mary and Zechariah, God uses angels to deliver His words to us. He speaks to us directly through words of encouragement and inspiration. Everything God has birthed inside you is blessed, and you are destined for greatness. Don't let the circumstances of how you discovered your destiny make you feel as though it's too soon or too late. There is nothing too hard for God. He is about to surprise you and everyone around you with what He can do.

Your heartache is someone else's hope. If you make it through, somebody else is going to make it through. Tell your story. Kim McManus6

You have suffered long enough, and God is positioning you for success and receiving His abundant blessings. None of the changes and progress that you've made have been in vain. Every scrap will bless someone else through the remarkable power of your testimony.

Now that you are healed, God wants to use you to help other women who need to hear your testimony of survival and how you overcame them. Your trauma is not wasted, and God will use it to show someone else the way out. You will find real happiness, true freedom, and closeness with God.

Be bold enough to take charge of your purpose. Figure out what you need so you can ask for something that fulfills your need. Take control of your life, understand what's going on inside you, and repurpose what's within to help you cope with the things outside of you. Write your vision for the future and see the bigger picture.

If you find yourself looking down at the road in front of you, find the strength to lift your sights back up and strive toward realizing your vision for the future. Stop focusing on your past mistakes and learn from them. Focus on the bright future ahead of you. Make a vision board, pray, have faith in God, and believe in yourself.

You made it! Through the trauma, the disappointment, the rejection, the pain, and the shame, you made it. You're here. You're still standing! You are a living, breathing, walking testimony. God is going to use you mightily to show His great strength and power. Hold your head high, and don't allow anyone to make you hang it in shame ever again. Those days are behind you, and Satan is under your feet. Walk boldly toward your hope, your destiny, and your purpose, knowing that God is walking right next to you and upholding you. Yield to His plan for your life, which is far better than anything you could ever choose or imagine for yourself. Who would've thought you would be here now, in this blessed place where the options are endless?

You can now dream bigger and achieve more, using your God-given gifts and talents and sharing your story in a way to uplift and inspire. Be proud of yourself and every accomplishment you have made. You deserve to celebrate your worth and take joy in the bright future ahead.

* * *

Re-create, revise, renew, repurpose. This is your season to re-create your life, to revise your missteps, to renew your strength, and repurpose your threads.

The Word of God provides for your re-creation.

"What happiness for those whose guilt has been forgiven! What joys when sins are covered over! What relief for those who have confessed their sins, and God has cleared their record."

(Psalm 32:1, The Living Bible).

It's a new season, my friend, and it's a new day. Dust off the dreams that hide in the deep crevices of your heart and re-create them. Stop seeing your missteps as stumbling blocks and consider them learning experiences. Rise from every broken place, and renew your hope, strength, vigor, and vitality. You can do this by the grace and favor of God.

Don't tuck the threads of your past experiences away, reluctant to tell anyone about what you have overcome. Repurpose your threads. They can be the very lifeline to connect another aching heart to the God of our salvation.

Change is hard for many people to accept. However, it's worth keeping in mind that growing as a person requires you to accept that life is continuously changing. We might lose our jobs or loved ones, relocate unexpectedly, or have other life-changing things happen to us, but these changes are part of life. We might not like how society or our community is changing, but we need to cope positively. Fortunately, there are many ways to view change, cope with it, and ultimately accept it.

Even over the course of reading this book, you've made many positive changes in your life. Don't be overwhelmed by them but see them as evidence of how God is moving in your life and molding you into the beautiful vessel, He created you to be. Don't stop where you are but continue to believe that God will do even more in you and through you because His work is not finished in you.

As you continue to make positive changes in your life, some people won't be able to make the shift with you. That's okay. Don't put new wine in an old wineskin; instead, trust that God is calling you to make the necessary changes. He has prepared the way for you to be successful. Let Him inspire you and connect you to your purpose, one positive change at a time.

Sometimes your dreams will seem scary as you ponder how and when they'll come to pass. You'll ask yourself:

Where will the money come from to start the business? Who's going to help me write the book? When will I get married? When will I have children? How long is it going to take me to do x, y, or z? Pace yourself and trust God. He will not give you all the answers at once, but He will give them to you when you need them and in His timing. If He told you everything, you'd have no reason to have faith.

Your trust in God is the substance that's going to sustain you through every season. If it doesn't happen as quickly as you thought or the way you would've liked it to happen, don't give up on God. Give Him a chance to iron out the details and work everything together for your good. Trust me, the end result will be worth the wait.

A Pattern to Quilt

Rise and step forward.

You were born to grow, so detach from anything and everything that attempts to keep you stuck in the same place. This is your season, this is your day, and this is your time to get up from the ashes and come out of the darkness. Emerge from your hiding place of shame and walk boldly. Don't look back but keep your eyes on God and the will He has for your life.

Develop yourself, your dreams, and your gifts. It's time to live your purpose and enjoy this incredible adventure God has for you.

Aren't you excited for what's next? Just think of where your life will take you in the next three months, six months, and a year. There's nothing too hard for God, and He moves timely! Know that you're beyond capable of making the biggest transformation of your life. To create the level of life you want, live out your purpose one day at a time, one moment at a time, and one good decision at a time.

You are the CEO of your life. You decide the thoughts that shape your reality. You decide who to

WELCOME, PROMOTE, DEMOTE, AND FIRE IN YOUR LIFE.

Give yourself room to believe and develop. Your life is your signature creation. It is your duty to live true to yourself. Your life's mission is to express yourself boldly, create what you love, love what you create, and enjoy the ride. It's about expanding and living your vision of yourself until it's the greatest possible expression of the One you represent.

A Prayer to Recreate

Father, Thank You so much for showing me that nothing I have experienced has been
in vain and that I do not have to be bound to the shame of my past.
Thank You for Your healing and redeeming power to not only set me free but to use
me to help set others free.
Thank You that Your plan and purpose for my life are good and that my destiny is
already prepared.
Even when I don't understand everything, I choose to allow You to use me for Your
glory, knowing that when my life is in Your hands
You work everything together for my good.
I am not a victim; I am a victor. I am beautiful, successful, and loved by You.
I look forward to the next step and the next phase of my life.
I will embrace this journey with an open mind and heart.
I will be positive and hopeful, knowing that I am worthy of blessings and prosperity.
Thank You for how You have opened my eyes to the truth about myself and whom
You made me to be.
In Jesus' name. Amen.

Reflect on Your Dreams

....
....
....
....
....
....
....
....
....
....
....
....
....
....
....
....
....
....
....
....
....

....
....
....
....
....
....
....
....
....
....
....
....
....
....
....
....
....
....
....
....
....
....
....
....

CONCLUSION

And we know that all things work together for good to those who love God, to those who are called according to His purpose."

(Romans 8:28, New King James Version).

What are our threads? They're the good, the bad, and the in-between parts of our life experiences that God weaves together for the good of our destiny. God the Father created us to be the manufacturers of our own lives. Jesus, the Son of God, calls and endorses us for service to God. And the Holy Spirit, our Comforter, is like the thread that weaves everything together for the kingdom at the appropriate time.

No matter where your life has taken you, no matter what traumatic experiences have happened to you, no matter where you find yourself right now, you can rest assured that God is at work within you, turning things around for your good and crafting a remarkable, beautiful, and inspiring masterpiece from the depths of your pain. He will fulfill His promise to give you hope and a future, and He will surely finish the good work that He started in you. There is nothing too hard for God, and you are a living testimony of His power and strength.

Every time you hear the voice of fear bullying you, telling you you're unworthy or unlovable,

---

Take a deep breath. With gentle love, remind your heart that love begins at the end of the last knot you made in your thread.

There's nothing wrong with feeling apprehensive regarding your future. However, embrace the unknown with excitement, and get ready to weave all the scraps of your life together to create an incredible experience through the grace and favor of God, using the "Power of 3":

Don't let the Enemy continue to use your trauma against you. You are a survivor, and he's not!

Don't put up walls to block Jesus and his shepherds. You are His daughter, and He loves you.

Don't waste your recovery from trauma. You've gained wisdom that can be used for the greater good.

It's time for you to release the trauma, unlock your potential, and fulfill what God has entrusted you to carry out along your journey. It's time for you to step up in your courage, disrupt and uproot what is holding you back, awaken the person and the spirit inside you, replant and grow your purpose, and emerge to make your impact.

According to 1 Peter 2:11, we are temporary residents and foreigners on the earth, so whatever happens to this body is just a part of our transition into eternity. Rape, incest, molestation, divorce, etc., are things someone can do to us, but they don't have to define or ruin us. You must believe this to be healed, using God as your shield.

A Call to Altar:

Think of the outcome you want to achieve

Harvest the lessons learned and heal your heart

Release fear and break the painful patterns

Enlist allies to become the person who has been locked inside

Adopt new mindsets and create new healthy patterns

Dream of a new you and design your joyful life

Some questions to reflect on after reading this book include:

What is my quilt going to look like once I use the threads of my experiences to construct my future?

Has the Enemy been controlling me with shame, unforgiveness, regret, anger, distrust?

Have I accepted Jesus into my life, asking Him to make me clean and whole again?

Looking beyond our brokenness, feelings of unworthiness, anger, and resentment, Christ meets us where we are. We already have God's approval and don't have to try to prove ourselves to gain acceptance from Him or anyone. God is unrelenting in His determination to help you. Trust God to work everything together for your good, and don't rush the process of healing.

Every piece of wooden furniture you sit on was once a small, insignificant seed that grew into a tree. That tree had to be cut down, milled, rebuilt, and sanded before it could become a piece of furniture. Can you allow God to take everything that seems insignificant in your life and build something that will stand the test of time?

Rest in the Lord and allow Him to heal you from the debilitating effects of trauma. Yes, you've gone through hell, but His strength can carry you and pull you from the darkness.

"Wait on the Lord; be of good courage, and He shall strengthen your heart."

(Psalm 27:14, New King James Version).

God can make you whole again, cleansing you, and renewing your spirit through Christ's sacrifice.

"There is therefore now no condemnation to those who are in

Christ Jesus"

(Romans 8:1, New King James Version).

Your troubled past can become a prosperous future.

"For I know the plans I have for you," declares the Lord, "plans to prosper you and not to harm you, plans to give you hope and a future."

(JEREMIAH 29:11, New International Version).

Ultimately, the hell you've been through can lead to an eternity in heaven.

For this is how much God loved the world—he gave his one and only unique Son as a gift. So now, everyone who believes in him will never perish but experience everlasting life. "God did not send his Son into the world to judge and condemn the world, but to be its Savior and rescue it!

John 3:16-17

You're made whole through the redeeming blood of Jesus. What can wash away the debilitating effects of sexual, physical, and emotional abuse? The blood of Jesus. What can make you pure and new again? The blood of Jesus. What will transform your life and give you the strength to rise to your purpose? The blood of Jesus. Your healing is within you because He is within you.

Your deliverance is already within you in the form of the Holy Spirit. Your breakthrough is within you. The Holy Spirit lives in every Christian to help and strengthen us. He can resurrect every gift and talent that you think has died. He will help you retrieve what's lost because He is a redeemer:

There are times when He presses us forward into prayer, into service, into suffering, into new experiences, new duties, new claims of faith, and hope, and love, but there are times when He arrests us in our activity and rests us under His overshadowing wing, and quiets us in the secret place of the Most High, teaching us some new lessons, breathing into us some deeper strength or fullness, and then leading us on again, at His bidding alone.[2]

This is not the time to relinquish your hope in the Lord because your healing hasn't manifested itself in the way you wanted or expected. Think of the shape of the cross. You have been up, down, across, beneath, below, and many positions in between, yet you survived the challenges that life threw at you. You're still here, and you're resilient because of it.

Your threads may have come unraveled, your life experiences may have left you with only scraps, and life may look messy and impossible to put back into any semblance of order, but God is a master craftsman. Turn to Him, and He will help you weave your scraps into a masterpiece.

Pray this prayer with me to be blessed in His healing.

CHAPTER 42

A Prayer for a Fresh Start

Father, I need You to renew a right spirit within me. I want to have the right spirit.
I'm tired of the hurt I'm carrying. I'm tired of being shackled to my past.
I want to be free. I want to be safe. I want to be a better woman.
Have mercy on me, my Lord, and make me whole.
Please, Lord, make me over again. I surrender everything to You—my heart, mind,
body, spirit, soul, and all my useless scraps.
I know you can use them and reshape them, for there is nothing too hard for You.
I'm ready to break with my past once and for all and start over from this day forward.
My past will no longer define me, and I want You to craft my destiny.
I want to walk in purpose and help others overcome through the power of my
testimony.
I am an overcomer. I am beautiful. I am loved and treasured by the King.
I am part of a royal priesthood.
Today is my new beginning. Today is my fresh start. Today I can and will be made
whole.
I thank You, Lord, for showing me who You are.
Thank You for being a Healer and a Waymaker.
Thank You for this brand- new day.
Thank You for creating a beautiful masterpiece out of all my life experiences.
In Jesus' name. Amen.

Go Forth with Your Quilt

Go forth and use your thread to stitch a better future.

Just like you, your quilt is fearfully and wonderfully made.

Don't hide the dark, messy threads that are underneath the surface, at the core of your being.

Every experience you've endured has made you who you are today and can be used for God's handy work.

Shine on. Shine brightly. Enjoy the adventure.

A Poem – Knitted to Perfection

We Are Strength
By Leonie H Mattison

Women are knitted to perfection,
Sharing a strong and unbound connection,
Stronger together through threads of affection,
God's strength and love become our reflection.

We break free from the trauma that confines,
We are transforming our scars into peace signs.
Reminding each other, we're beautiful,
For when we stand together, we become unmovable.

"The grace of the Lord Jesus Christ and the love of God and

the fellowship of the Holy Spirit be with you all."

(2 Corinthians 13:14).

May you allow the Lord advance and evolve you beyond your trauma

Detailed Steps

STEP 1: T-THINK

Think of The Outcome You Want to Achieve.
Ask yourself:

- Who do I want to be?
- What outcome do I want to achieve?
- What does "this woman" look like?

STEP 2: H-HARVEST

Harvest the Lessons Learned and Heal Your Heart.
Ask yourself:

- What have I learned from the past about my decision making?
- Do I have a system or process I use to make decisions?
- What knowledge gained can I use from my past to forge a new path forward?

STEP 3: R-RELEASE

Release Fear and Break the Painful Patterns.
Ask yourself:

- Am I taking steps to become the woman I say I want to be?
- Do I think good things about myself?
- Is there anything about me I need to change?
- Am I keeping my commitment to myself?

STEP 4: E-ENLIST

**Enlist Allies to Become the Person
Who Has Been Locked Inside. Ask yourself:**

- Who in my life can I enlist to support me?
- Do I need to have an impartial person to work with?
- Would I benefit from a coach, mentor, counselor, or therapist to help me work through different challenges?
- What workshops or books will support my vision?

STEP 5: A-ADOPT

**Adopt New Mindsets and Create New Healthy Patterns.
Ask yourself:**

- What new habit do I want to start?
- What old habit do I want to break?
- How can I think differently?

STEP 6: D-DREAM

**Dream of A New You and Design Your Joyful Life.
Ask yourself:**

- What life do I really want?
- What is the first step I need to take to bring my vision to life?
- Who am I six to twelve months from today?
- Then, take action.

21 Self-Care Ideas

1. **Encourage yourself**: The fact that you've survived whatever you've faced is enough to acknowledge your effort and celebrate the progress you've made. Do your best to be loyal to yourself in times when you feel defeated. Be there for yourself. You need to be able to count on your- self and to believe in yourself. Treat yourself and speak to yourself the way you would a good friend. Encourage yourself using the Word of God.

2. **Smile**: A real smile can quickly and naturally lift your spirits. It's like you're showing no fear and that, despite your circumstances, you'll be happy because you have Jesus on your side. Smiling also contributes to longevity, as it helps increase your well-being and general happiness. Smiling makes you more likable and courteous, which yields beautiful results for yourself and others.

3. **Laugh**: While smiling boosts your happiness, laughing is a physical manifestation that your situation does not perturb you because you know the one called "Abba Father." Like Sarah, with laughter, you can boldly say God has your back. "God has made laughter for me; everyone who hears will laugh over me" (Genesis 21:6). Some of the simple ways I brought laughter back into my life after Bell's palsy were to watch funny videos online and on DVDs, tune in to my favorite sitcoms and plays, listen to some comedy on the radio, and read jokes and quotes of the day. I also read entertaining children's books while spending time with my daughter.

4. **Play**: Dwelling on your present situation will keep you feeling sad, worried, and stressed, but tapping into your inner child can take your mind off your troubles. One of my friends encouraged me to volunteer in the toddler classroom at the preschool where I worked. This was a breakthrough in my healing process. One child asked if I was now the class clown. I told her, yes, and every afternoon for one hour, I changed out of my work clothes into a red clown suit and allowed twenty toddlers the joy of my crooked smile for thirty minutes. It was painful for me to flex my facial muscles, but seeing these innocent children take joy in something I thought was so painful made me smile from the inside out. For the first time, I noticed that something good could come from my pain.

5. **Get creative**: Creativity is a powerful way we craft new and beautiful things. So, even when your situation feels out of control, harnessing your creativity will inspire you to make something wonderful. Coloring, painting, sewing, making crafts, and writing are all ways to create something you can be proud of. They allow you to put your difficult situation on the back burner.

6. Some of the world's greatest masterpieces have been borne out of pain, such as the paintings from Picasso's blue period. If you're having trouble stirring up your

creativity, you can do something as simple as coloring. It's not just for kids; there are beautiful adult coloring books that have been shown to reduce stress and anxiety. I have also designed an adult coloring book to help bring peace, healing, and restoration to your life and a profound closeness with God.

7. **Eat well and rest**: Except when we're fasting, it's not recommended that we go without food. Situations can make us lose our appetite, but eating healthy food is what gives us the physical ammunition to restore our body. In the Bible, Paul suggested this to the people on a sinking ship with him when they were afraid: "Therefore, I urge you to take some food. For it will give you strength, for not a hair is to perish from the head of any of you." (Acts 27:34). During my recovery from Bell's palsy and before I could eat solid food again, soups, mashed potatoes, avocadoes, and coconut water became my best friends. But I was careful not to binge-eat. Besides feeding the body with the right foods, I encourage you to carve out meaningful time to exercise and rest, one of the best ways to rejuvenate and restore a well-nourished body. In doing so, the seed of healing took root in my heart, and color began to come back to my cheeks. I was smiling again and have been smiling ever since.

8. **Give**: Giving to and investing in others is a sure way of taking the focus off yourself. Doing this will bring you inner joy and fulfillment as well. I loved giving to others while I was recovering because blessing others helped me see that it wasn't all about me. I started writing short inspirational messages and daily texted them to my girlfriends, encouraging them to build their faith in God. In doing so, I, too, was inspired. As I did this, God, through His Holy Spirit, kept whispering into my spirit promises so grand that my faith grew as tall as a mountain.

9. **Practice self-care**: You need appropriate time for healing and recovery to be your best self. Self-care is not selfish; it's a vital part of the healing process. Self-care can be as simple as a warm bath or as extravagant as going to the spa. Take some time to focus on loving and nurturing yourself. Daily, I would affirm, "I now release with joy every sickness, every disease, every pain, and every misaligned emotion from my body. I bless with love my being and welcome with joy my well-being. My body is healed, and I appreciate my body parts for their support in helping me to fulfill my purpose." I still do that today. Love and appreciate the body God has blessed you with.

10. **Forgive**: Forgiving yourself, and others give you a peace that cannot be found in physical possessions or activities. Because I blamed myself for past painful experiences, I had to release the blame and regret, knowing that it wasn't my fault. I also had to forgive everyone who had looked down on and talked about me because of my condition. Release the negative emotions and burdens that come from guilt and hurt.

11. **Embrace peace**: It doesn't matter how loud the noise around you is; make sure it's not more audible inside you. Watch over your heart, for from it flow the springs of life (Proverbs 4:23 NASB). Protect the personal peace of your heart, for, in the absence of peace, turmoil abounds. But when you know the truth, the truth will set you free. Let His peace wash over you, cleansing away your doubt, fear, and anxiety.

12. **Activate your faith**: I spent many days in isolation and hopelessness. I began praying, reading, reciting God's Word, and giving thanks, activating my faith in God's power to heal me of this illness, just like the woman with the issue of blood. Jeremiah 17:14 became one of my favorite prayers: "Heal me, LORD, and I will be healed; save me, and I will be saved, for you are the one I praise" (NIV).

13. **Create a fantastic space of love**: Share love often and willingly. You don't need to go into anyone's darkness to help them. The only way to lead others out of darkness is to hold your light high to see their way out.

14. **Reflect**: Take some time to reflect on what got you here without blaming yourself or judging yourself. It's okay to hold yourself accountable and identify the behaviors that will help you to make better decisions in the future. Don't allow yourself or the Enemy to weigh you down with what you wish you had done differently. Always speak as encouragingly to yourself as you would to a dear friend going through trauma.

15. **Take Epsom salt baths**: I take Epsom salt baths, hugging myself and pampering myself with lotion to be therapeutic. I also practice praying the Word of God over my life and speaking these words of truth over my body, "I love you," reminding my soul that "God loves you more" and "You are enough." Know that you can and will make it through this and walk into your much brighter future with God. Determine that you are a changed person and that from this point forward, you will protect and assert yourself.

16. **Decide today that your past will not define you**: Use these life threads to help others get through their trauma, too. Rise above the temptation to give up or feel as though there's no hope left. If you have breath in your body, you have an opportunity to override every circumstance that makes you think life isn't worth living anymore. You have a chance now to use the power God has invested in you to take control of your life, take back your joy, and share it with the world.

17. **Develop a strong devotional life**: If you have thoughts of leaving the church due to the spiritual abuse you've experienced, don't be ashamed. This is an entirely normal reaction. At one point, I walked away from the church because it was difficult for me to trust God. I blamed Him and the clergy, who were a representation of Him. It wasn't until after I started processing the trauma that I could begin my relationship with God anew.

18. **Choose to pursue a deeper relationship with God**: Recognize that His love will deliver you from the shame of your past. He will give you the strength and courage to overcome your defeat and to come out of the darkness once and for all. Through understanding who God is and how much He loves you, you'll find the ability to love and forgive yourself and your abuser(s).

19. **Refuse to play the victim**: God doesn't want us to walk around with the shame of what we've done or what's happened to us. He came to set the captives free, so let His redeeming power expel all guilt and shame from you. God knows the end from the beginning. Over time, you'll be able to separate your abuser from God and the church. God doesn't want to see you in pain. He wants to restore you and show you that He is sovereign, even in your tragedy.

20. **Remember, this isn't a journey you have to walk alone**: Many resources, such as counseling, are available. The effects of abuse are damaging and isolating, and they invade every aspect of your life mentally, emotionally, spiritually, and physically. The effects remain long after the abuse has ended. It's therefore crucial for you to work through these emotions so they won't have power over you or keep you from fulfilling your purpose in Christ.

21. **Allow God to help you to overcome**: You are not too broken to be healed. God loves you, and He wants you to heal and thrive beyond that abuse you've experienced. Rest in the Lord!

22. **Love yourself**: You are love! You were created in love and by love. Stay in the presence of God's genuine love, for His unconditional love will fill you up continually

Frequently Asked Questions

What is the Book About?

The Thread is my life story, a childhood knitted together with adverse, severe experiences that left me with posttraumatic stress disorder, a prisoner in my soul, and trapped in my mind. As a single mother of three, when I looked at myself in the mirror, I saw myself as a broken girl with a sick soul, a noisy mind, and a broken heart.

The Thread was born out of these life-shattering circumstances. In a tapestry of stories, I share my struggles, pairing them with tales of fifteen women in the Bible who also faced severe tragedy, trial, or failure. I lead readers along a gentle path that shows them how these women responded in faith and explain "the thread" is created in each of them. The result is a resounding call to action.

The women of The Thread dare to discover, embrace, and accelerate their God-given purpose. My prayer is that each beloved reader will recognize that they, too, are worthy of love, can find freedom, and enjoy closeness with God.

Why Did you Write the Book?

My main hope was to create a solution that could help women free themselves from being the woman who trauma created. So, I focused on inviting readers into my journey of trauma, sufferings, and faith with loads of vulnerability, bravery, and honesty. This is not an indictment of the Christian church or any church. It is not a vehicle to seek revenge for past wrongs (no matter how horrible), nor is it meant to undermine men or men in ministry. This book is all about healing.

The circumstances I have written about are an important part of my story, but the names of individuals have been changed, characters have been combined for brevity, and locations have been switched to protect the innocent and any other victims who have chosen not to be identified.

I hope to bring people inside the experience of a girl who endured Adverse Childhood Experiences, or ACEs, whose life has been radically transformed by the power of God, and how she became the woman who's helping individuals, teams and organizations achieve intentional transformation. My prayer is that the stories, the sharing of my life story, will empower you to release your story and allow God to transform your brokenness into a life-sized breakthrough.

Who is the book written for?

Women who have suffered trauma and are left in the dark, silenced by guilt, shame, and the overwhelming burden of blame that society often places on the victim.

Organizations and individuals working to end abuse, as well as men who are interested in gaining a better understanding of the impact of severe trauma, will get an insight into how they can better support and love people through and beyond trauma.

How will women overcome trauma?

As a result of the six-step THREAD system where women usually feel unworthy, damaged, and humiliated, they might begin to feel whole, at peace, happy, and complete, as a Daughter of God. I see women living a brand-new life as overcomers with no limitations on who, how, and what they can become in God. They are living an abundant life in Christ and have even launched careers that are positively impacting the world.

The steps of The Thread, when followed, will allow women to:

Step 1: **Think** of the Outcome They Want to Achieve

Step 2: **Harvest** the Lessons They've Learned and Heal Their Heart

Step 3: **Release** Trauma, Choose Courage, and Reclaim Their Life

Step 4: **Enlist** Allies to Becoming the Person who has Been Locked Inside

Step 5: **Adopt** New Mindsets to Break the Painful Patterns and Create New Healthy

Behaviors

Step 6: **Dream** of A New You and Design Your Joyful Life

REFERENCES

Section 1

1. World Health Organization. Violence Against Women. 29, 2017, https://www.who.int/health-topics/violence-against-women#tab=tab_1
2. Same as above
3. Centers for Disease Control and Prevention. **About the CDC-Kaiser ACE Study | Violence Prevention | Injury Center | CDC.** Centers for Disease Control and Prevention. April 13, 2020. https://www.cdc.gov/violenceprevention/aces/about.html.
4. **Connections Between Faith Communities and Their Non-Profits.** PilotStudyFindingsReport.pdf. Accessed September 29, 2019. https://www.sp2.upenn.edu/wp-content/uploads/2018/02/

Section 2

1. Blue. Ken. **Healing Spiritual Abuse How to Break Free from Bad Church Experiences.** Downers Grove, Illinois: InterVarsity Press, 1993, 12.
2. Ryan, Juanita, and Dale. **Recovery from Spiritual Abuse:** 6 Studies for Groups or Individuals (Downers Grove, Illinois: InterVarsity Press, 1992), 15.
3. Carolyn Custis James. **Standing Up to Spiritual Abusers.** Carolyn Custis James, May 30, 2017, carolyncustisjames.com/2013/07/10/ standing-up-to-spiritual-abusers/.
4. Ibid.
5. Psychology Today. **Why Agreement to Sex Is Not Consent.** Sussex Publishers. Accessed December 19, 2019. https://www.psychologyto-day.com/us/blog/the-mysteries-love/201803/ why-agreement-sex-is-not-consent.
6. Ibid.
   Varin, J. **About This Site. I Kissed Church Goodbye,** March 17, 2014. https://jvarin.wordpress.com/about/.
7. **Hagar: Scriptural Patterns of Sexual Assault.** The Exponent, May 12, 201. www.the-exponent.com/ hagar-scriptural-patterns-of-sexual-assault/.
8. Arthur, Kay. **Quote: Snuggle in God's Arms. When You Are Hurting, When You Feel Lonely, Left Out.** Inspiring Quotes. Accessed December 19, 2019. https://www.inspiringquotes.us/ quotes/tSvk_1moSpGbr.
9. David E. and Diana R. Garland. **Flawed Families of the Bible: How God's Grace Works through Imperfect Relationships** (Ada, Michigan: Brazos

Press, 2007), 23.

10. Ibid, 25.
11. Ibid.
12. Ibid.
13. Coventry, Petrina. **Understanding the Psychology of Power Abuse.** business.com. business.com, April 23, 2018. https://www.business.com/articles/ psychology-of-power-abuse/.
14. Tabatha Coffey Quotes. BrainyQuote. Xplore. Accessed September 29, 2019. https://www.brainyquote. com/quotes/tabatha_coffey_657328.
15. F. Remy Diederich. **How to Recover from Spiritual Abuse.** F. Remy Diederich, September 20, 2017. www. readingremy.com/how-to-recover-from-spiritual-abuse/.

Section 3

1. Got Questions. **How Could Jacob Not Notice He Married Leah Instead of Rachel?** GotQuestions.org, January 25, 2018. www. gotquestions.org/Leah-and-Rachel.html.
2. Chuck McKnight, **Jacob's Marriage to Leah, Rachel, Bilhah & Zilpah. Patheos,** November 15, 2017, www. patheos.com/blogs/hippieheretic/2017/11/jacobs-mar- riage-to-leah-rachel-bilhah-zilpah.html.
3. Laughter Online. University. **How to Practice Ho'oponopono in Four Simple Steps.** 6 Dec. 2018, www.laughteron- lineuniversity.com/hooponopono-4-simple-steps/.

Section 4

1. Coleman, Alison. **How A Near-Fatal Car Crash Inspired An Italian Entrepreneur's Mind-Boosting Business Idea.** Forbes. Forbes Magazine, July 11, 2016. https://www.forbes.com/sites/alisoncoleman/2016/07/10/how-a-near-fatal-car-crash-inspired-a- mind-boosting-business-idea.
2. Schweitzer, Albert. **A Quote by Albert Schweitzer.** Goodreads. Goodreads. Accessed September 29, 2019. https://www. goodreads.com/quotes/12028-in-everyone-s-life-at- some-time-our-inner-fire-goes.

Section 5

1. **Pistis - New Testament Greek Lexicon - King James Version.**

https://www.biblestudytools.com/lexi- cons/greek/kjv/pistis.html

2. Graham. Billy. **A Quote from Billy Graham in Quotes. Goodreads Meet Your Next Favorite Book.** Accessed December 7, 2019. https://www.goodreads.com/quotes/7474998- faith-isn-t-pretending-our-problems-don-t-exist-nor-is-it.

3. Angelou, Maya. **Letter to My Daughter. London:** Virago, 2014, 4.

4. Goodreads. **A Quote from Overcoming Life's Obstacles.** Goodreads. Accessed September 29, 2019. https://www.goodreads.com/quotes/784072- encour- age-yourself-believe-in-yourself-and-love-yourself-never- doubt.

5. Melanie Curtin. **Neuroscience Says Doing This 1 Thing Makes You Just as Happy as Eating 2,000 Chocolate Bars.** Inc.com, August 29, 2017, www.inc.com/melanie-curtin/science-says-doing-this-makes-you-just-as-happy-as.html.

6. Haden, Jeff. **Top 350 Inspiring Motivational Quotes to Tweet and Share.** Inc.com. Inc., October 10, 2014. https://www.inc.com/jeff-haden/top-350-inspiring-mo- tivational-quotes-to-tweet-and-share.html.

Section 6

1. Ministry Today. **Tommy Are You Dreaming BIG Enough?** Ministry Today, February 28, 2005. ministrytodaymag.com/ leadership/vision/10649-are-you-dreaming-big-enough.

2. Ibid.

3. Tubman, Harriet. **A Quote by Harriet Tubman.** Goodreads. Goodreads. Accessed September 29, 2019. https://www.goodreads. com/quotes/5935-every-great-dream-begins-with-a- dreamer-always-remember-you.

4. Goodreads. **A Quote from Love Is Letting Go of Fear.** Goodreads. Accessed September 29, 2019. https://www. goodreads.com/quotes/314269-inner-peace-can-be- reached-only-when-we-practice-forgiveness.

5. Arthur, Kay. **Quotes (Author of Lord, I Want to Know You).** Goodreads. Goodreads. Accessed September 29, 2019. https://www.goodreads.com/author/ quotes/4170.Kay_Arthur.

6. Bell, C. **A Quote by C. JoyBell C.** Goodreads. Goodreads. Accessed September 29, 2019. https://www.goodreads. com/quotes/360492-the-only-person-who-can-pull-me- down-is-myself.

Section 7

1. All Gifts. **Definition of Gifts.** Gifts Test, https://giftstest.com/ allgifts.

2. Billy Graham, **Discover Your God-given Gift and Use It for His Glory.** Billy Graham Evangelistic Association,September 13, 2016,

billygraham.org/answer/ discover-your-god-given-gift-and-use-it-for-his-glory/.
3. **A Quote from A Man After God's Own Heart.** Goodreads. Goodreads. Accessed September 29, 2019. https://www.goodreads.com/quotes/949772-start- where-you-are-do-anything-you-can-do-and-do.
4. Crystal Lutton, **Deborah the Judge and Jael the Just.** CBE International, June 22, 2016. www.cbeinternational. org/blogs/deborah-judge-and-jael-just.
5. Bernock, Danielle. **What Are Spiritual Gifts? Understanding the Types and Discovering Yours.** Christianity.com. Salem Web Network, May 8,2019. https://www.christianity.com/christian-life/what-are-spiritual-gifts-understanding-the-types-and-dis- covering-yours.html.
6. Roberts, Sarah Jakes. **Don't Settle for Safe: Embracing the Uncomfortable to Become Unstoppable.** Place of publication not identified: Thomas Nelson PUB, 2018. Page 27

Section 8

1. Richard Tedeschi, PhD, and Lawrence Calhoun, PhD, Journal of Traumatic Stress, 1996
2. Psychology Today. **Can Suffering Make Us Stronger?** Psychology Today. Sussex Publishers. Accessed September 29, 2019. https://www.psychologytoday. com/us/blog/out-the-darkness/201111/can-suffering-make-us-stronger.
3. Rendon, Jim. **How Trauma Can Change You-For the Better.** Time. Time, July 22, 2015. https://time.com/3967885/how-trauma-can-change-you-for-the-better.
3. **Dweck, Carole. Learn the Differences between Fixed and Growth Mindset from 'Mindset: How You Can Fulfil Your Potential.** The Insider Tales, August 5, 2017. www.theinsidertales.com/learn-differences-be- tween-fixed-growth-mindset-from-mindset-how-you- can-fulfil-your-potential-by-carol-dweck/.
4. Myer, Joyce. **Trusting God When You Don't Understand. The Christian Post.** The Christian Post, August 5, 2014. https://www.christianpost.com/news/ trusting-god-when-you-dont-understand.html.
5. Quote Collection Project. **Your Heartache Is Someone Else's Hope. If You Make It through, Somebody Else Is Going to Make It through. Tell Your Story.** May 22, 2013. https://quo-tecollectionproject.tumblr.com/post/51030514519/ your-heartache-is-someone-elses-hope-if-you-make.
6. Quote Collection Project. **Your Heartache Is Someone Else's Hope. If You Make It through, Somebody Else Is Going to Make It through. Tell Your Story.** May 22, 2013. https://quo-tecollectionproject.tumblr.com/post/51030514519/ your-heartache-is-

someone-elses-hope-if-you-make

Conclusion

1. Warren, Rick. **The Purpose-Driven Life: What on Earth Am I Here for?** Grand Rapids, MI: Zondervan, 2016.
2. Romans 8:25 NASB: **But if we hope for what we do not see, with perseverance we wait eagerly for it.** Accessed September 29, 2019. https://biblehub.com/nasb/ romans/8-25.htm.

Appendix 1

Trauma Resources List

Trauma is easier to cope with when we have support, so I've compiled a partial list of resources in this appendix. The inclusion of selected resources does not necessarily signify my endorsement.

Crisis Intervention Hotlines

• National Suicide Prevention Lifeline 1-800-273-TALK (8255)

• The National Runaway Switchboard 1-800-RUNAWAY (786-2929)

• National Domestic Violence Hotline: 800-799-7233

• National Sexual Assault Online Hotline

• Crisis Link 24/7 regional hotline: 703-527-4077

• Domestic Violence Program: 24-hour hotline: 703-838-4911

Resources for Survivors of Abuse

• Survivors of Incest Anonymous

• RAINN (the Rape, Abuse & Incest National Network)

• Great list

Resources for Sexual Addictions

• Sexual Compulsives Anonymous

• Sex Addicts Anonymous

• Sex and Love Addicts Anonymous (SLAA)

- Sexaholics Anonymous

  - Am I a sex addict?

- The Recovery Zone (SAST, SARA, and PSS assessment tools located here)

Resources for Drug/Alcohol Addiction and Recovery

- Alcoholics Anonymous

- Al-Anon

- Al-Ateen

- Adult Children of Alcoholics

- Women for Sobriety

- SMART Recovery

Resources for Traumatic Stress, PTSD and Dissociation

- The Sidran Foundation

- The Trauma Centre

Resources for Self-Care

- Self-Compassion

- Tara Brach: Meditation, Emotional Healing, and Spiritual Awakening

- Health Journeys

Resources for Self-Injurious Behavior

- S.A.F.E. Alternatives

Resources for Eating Disordered Behaviors

- National Eating Disorders Association

- Something Fishy

• Eating Disorder Network of Maryland

Resources for Separation, Divorce, and Re-marriage

• The Divorce Center

• Divorce Mediation

• Children and Divorce

• Step Families

• The Collaborative Divorce

Therapeutic Associations/Organizations

• PACT Institute

• American Association of Marriage and Family Therapy (AAMFT)

• EMDR International Association (EMDRIA)

• The Society for the Advancement of Sexual Health (SASH)

• Mid Atlantic Association for IMAGO Relationship Therapists (MAIT)

• Imago Relationship Therapy

• Sensorimotor Psychotherapy Institute (SPI)

• International Centre For Excellence in Emotionally Focused Therapy (ICEEFT)

• International Society for the Study of Trauma and Dissociation (ISSTD)

Resources for Survivors of Spiritual Abuse

• The Hope of Survivors

• Spiritual Abuse Resources

• American Association of Christian Counselors

• The Ancient Paths by Craig Hill

Appendix 2

Tip for Parents

Parents, you must talk to your daughters about feeling secure and being free to say, "No." Remind them that they have free will to sexual advances and understanding the difference between consensual sexual intercourse and 'sexual abuse. Don't force your children to hug or to kiss anyone that they don't want. This will reinforce the importance of valuing one's self. It is also important to help your sons understand what rape and non-consent mean and that they can and must say "No," to unwelcomed situations.

A parent's silence will hurt rather than protect their children. Create a safe environment so that your children can come to you to share concerns or anxieties they may have about anyone and to ask for help. Put a system in place, such as an established code word they can use if they encounter sexual assault. For more information, visit: https://www.rainn.org/articles/ talking-your-kids-about-sexual-assault

Also, ensure that the place where you practice faith and where you contribute your gifts and talents has balanced teaching from the pulpit and policies and procedures to provide the ethical treatment of women. This might be an uncomfortable subject to broach considering the lack of discourse around the topic in church environments, but only by talking about abuse and consent openly and honestly can we hope to effect change.

What should churches do to prevent sexual abuse?

I want to encourage every faith-based organization, faith leaders, members of the congregation, and boards to take steps to reduce the likelihood of child sexual abuse. Implementing an ongoing sexual abuse prevention training program to paid employees, volunteers, and members of the congregation can help provide a safe and secure environment for children to whom the faith community has been entrusted and help reduce the legal risk and liability. The purpose is not to provoke panic but to set a new and higher standard, raise awareness of abuse, and provide educational information for prevention and intervention.

According to LifeWay.com, www.MinistrySafe.com provides unique resources for church ministry programs, including:

- Sexual Abuse Awareness Training for staff members and volunteers

- Sample forms for applications, references, and interviews as part of the Skillful Screening Process

- Safety Policy and Procedures tailored to various ministry programs that dovetail with Sexual Abuse Awareness Training

- Background Checks adapted by the client to fit the position

- The MinistrySafe online Control Panel, giving administrators the ability to monitor the easily 5-Part Safety System

Other Resources

- https://www.stopitnow.org/
- https://protectmyministry.com/Child-Safety-Training/

ABOUT THE AUTHOR

Dr. Leonie H Mattison knows what keeps most survivors of trauma and those living in crisis feeling unworthy and not living the life they deserve because she's been there! Leonie spent many days with the burden of guilt, trauma, shame, and self-loathing until she learned there was another way. And since then, she has never looked back. She now knows, identifying, applying, and practicing the art of intentional living, should never be an afterthought. It should be a daily endeavor, and she guides you through using the power of intentionality to choose the desired outcome you want to achieve in every situation.

As an Organizational and Talent Development Practitioner, Motivational Speaker, and Author of The Thread collection, Dr. Mattison has dedicated her career to transforming lives through high-quality education, cutting-edge research, and people-centric leadership. She is an adjunct graduate and undergraduate professor, student advisor, and mentor, and her 23 years career spans nonprofits, government, and the private sector, building strong leaders and high-performing teams. She has a strong track record of increasing employee engagement and cultivating continuous learning cultures that inspire people to achieve measurable organizational outcomes. Leonie is adept at leading concurrent projects, teams, and initiatives, impacting up to 60 departments, 26,000 employees, and 8.4 million constituents. An entrepreneurial fundraiser with a successful track record of securing and administering budgets and grant awards up to $45 million.

On a personal level, Leonie has overcome many of life's worst challenges, including a series of adverse childhood experiences, severe bouts of Bell's Palsy, a near-death Stroke, a difficult failed marriage, and a close fatal suicide attempt. Leonie has a fantastic story of how God transformed her traumatic life experiences into an ordained purpose. As an international speaker, her women empowerment workshops, learning programs, and resources are filled with hopeful life lessons to empower women to break free from unhealthy relationships and behaviors that make them feel unworthy or undeserving and win back their power.

Her infectious energy, coupled with her engaging, uplifting, and educational - six-step T.H.R.E.A.D System©, aims to empower women achieve intentional transformation. As a motivational "arsonist," her presentations "fire you up" with concrete ideas to help you discover your worth, embrace an intentional mindset and make your dreams a reality. As a "Get Intentional" expert, her core belief is based upon "being intentional is the key to achieving success at work, in school, at home, and in life."

Her core belief is, **"transformed people transform others to impact the world."**

Further Work and Educational Experiences

Dr. Mattison is currently serving as the Chief of Organizational and Talent Development division at the County of Santa Barbara (C.O.S.B.). Under her leadership, the C.O.S.B.'s training center has transformed into an accredited Employees' University, offering its 4,000+ workforce access to graduate and undergraduate degrees and high-quality learning programs.

Before joining COSB, Dr. Mattison served in leadership roles as Sansum Diabetes Director of Clinical Research Operations and Major Grants, New York City Department of Health and Mental Hygiene's Public Health Research Grant Administrator, Newark Alliance Workforce and Economic Development Program Officer, and Merck Pharmaceutical Continuing Medical Education Coordinator and Business Analyst.

DISCLAIMER

The information provided in *The Thread collection* is offered for educational and informational purposes solely, and it is made available to you as a self-help tool for your use. Reasonable care is taken to ensure that the information presented is accurate to the best of the Author's knowledge, views, and belief.

Before going further, I need to categorically state that this book is not an indictment of the Christian church or any church. It is not a vehicle to seek revenge for past wrong (no matter how horrible), nor is it meant to undermine men or men in ministry. This book is strictly about healing and drawing closer to God than you have ever imagined possible. This book is written with a focus on the many waves of abuse women suffer (physical, mental, sexual, and spiritual), but it can also be used by anyone who wants to overcome shadows from the past that are holding them back.

The Thread collection is designed to help you cope in your present life right now after the trauma. The author does not ask you to think about the traumatic experience itself or its details. However, some of the stories and exercises in this book may call up powerful unpleasant memories accompanied by overwhelming feelings. One of this book's first tasks is to teach you how to guard your heart should this happen. The author offers tools to help you along your healing journey later in the book. For this reason, you are encouraged to read through the prologue and the first five chapters of this book in sequence. Don't skip ahead until you are sure you have ways to take care of yourself when strong feelings arise.

The circumstances the author has written about or share publicly are an important part of her story. But the names of individuals have been changed, characters have been combined for brevity, and locations have been switched to protect the innocent and any other victims who have chosen not to be identified. The author added undeniable examples of God's ability to transform those horrible experiences into a beautiful quilt that would glorify His love, power, and personal care

The information in *The Thread collection* is not intended to be a substitute for professional medical advice, diagnosis, or treatment that can be provided by your own Medical

Provider (including doctor/physician, nurse, physician's assistant, or any other health professional), Mental Health Provider (including psychiatrist, psychologist, therapist, counselor, or social worker), or member of the clergy.

Therefore, do not disregard or delay seeking professional medical, mental health, or religious advice because of information you have read from the author either through her books, online resources, online coaching, mentoring, post, or speaking sessions. Do not stop taking any medications without speaking to your own Medical Provider or Mental Health Provider. If you have or suspect that you have a medical or mental health problem, contact your own Medical Provider or Mental Health Provider promptly.

Sew

Your Best Life Tapestry with Intention

If variety is the spice of life, then your vibrant life threads are the ingredients of the recipe that make you who you are.

Love,

Your Sister in Intentional Transformation

Made in the USA
Las Vegas, NV
18 December 2020